I0788591

DARK FAE FREED

BROKEN COURT BOOK TWO

HEATHER RENEE

CONTENTS

To Nat Navarro,
Thank you for loving my books almost as much as I do! You
are a rockstar!

CHAPTER 1

Fury fueled my every thought and movement as I continued forward. It didn't matter that I had been knocked on my ass. I had a singular goal, and nothing would distract me from what needed to be done. Not even the wounds covering my body.

I might have been broken, but I wasn't giving up.

The further I flew from Finn's farm, the more my emotions came back to me, but not in the way I'd felt them before. I was once again the monster the king had created. Except this time, Zephyr was my target. My intent was ruthless. My care was gone. Nothing mattered beyond killing *him*.

He'd shown up moments after I'd blown Edgar to bits, hopefully to never be put back together. Perfect timing on the king's part, likely thanks to Dain, the son nobody knew the king had and whose death I had zero remorse about. He'd been a traitorous fae who ended up being more devious than I'd thought possible.

With a destination clear in my mind, I teleported myself mid-flight and landed on the pristine beaches of West Island. I knew King Zephyr wouldn't have gone anywhere but his fortress. Unfortunately for him, it wouldn't remain a fortress for long.

My feet pounded against the sand as I drew on my power, willing the magic within me to heal the wounds I'd suffered. Between the fight with Edgar and the hits the king had gotten in before disappearing, I knew the damage to my body was extensive, especially to my left wing. I could still use it for the basics, though, and I wouldn't let a bit of pain stop me.

Nothing can stop us, my inner voice hissed as magic began to trickle from my fingers and wrap around my arms and wings.

With every step, my bones began to heal and muscles regained their strength. I wasn't at my best, but it didn't matter. My drive to see this through would be enough. I had to stay on task. I would find and end King Zephyr, no matter the consequences.

By the time I arrived at the gate, my wings were extended and turned back into hardened weapons while magic swirled around me like the rage I carried deep within me.

At some point, either during the previous fight or on my flight over, my braid had come halfway undone. Instead of trying to fix the tangled mess, I untied the rest and let my iridescent strands fly behind me as my steps brought me closer to the one thing I wanted most.

One of the fae guards caught sight of me and began yelling, but I didn't let him get more than two words out. With a dozen lethal feathers already in hand, I sent one sailing toward his throat.

He didn't react quickly enough, and blood gushed from the wound as his fingers helplessly tried to cover the gash. By the time I reached him, the guard was on his knees, gurgling incoherent words. I paid him no attention as I continued forward.

A line of nearly a dozen guards waited by the water well, and another smaller row beyond that. The good thing about seeing what waited for me was that it proved King Zephyr was indeed afraid of me and somewhere within his castle.

"If you stop now, the king just might show you some mercy, Lucinda," Gabriel shouted from the castle gates, hiding behind the rows of fae like a coward.

He'd been even more ruthless than King Zephyr when I lived here. I hadn't forgotten the times he'd nearly drowned me, whipped my back until there wasn't an inch of skin untouched, or when he'd made me wear the blood of those I'd killed when I was only thirteen.

If it was possible, Gabriel might have been even more vile than the king. He didn't deserve a verbal response.

A wave of magic surged from my hands and into the first line of guards, followed closely by several more of my feathers. My power burned the skin of my opponents, and the feathers sunk deep into their chests. Only half of the guards were left, and I was just getting started.

Five fae came charging toward me at once, but I

wasn't going to give up, no matter how dire things might seem. Power blasted into me, and my wings acted as a shield, absorbing the impact. Waiting until the king's pawns were within physical striking distance, I flung my wings out and sliced three of their heads off in one strike.

Another guard snuck around behind me at some point and tackled me, wrapping his arms around my waist while another guard stepped on my wings, standing over my head. Ignoring the searing pain from the magic of the one restraining me, I jerked my arm up and grabbed on to the junk of the one above me.

With one pull, he came down, freeing my wings and nearly sitting on my face, knocking the other guard away. We rolled around on the ground, and I used my feet to kick him backward. Before I could get up, the previous guard moved back in and sliced a blade across my stomach, leaving a gash that wouldn't heal anytime soon.

Damn it!

I groaned, soaking in the agony and turning it to rage, then swiveled around and cut my attacker's chest open with my wings, enjoying the gasp of surprise coming from the fae who thought he had bested me. *Not today, asshole.*

Even with five down in a matter of minutes, I was nowhere close to getting inside the castle. I called my power forth once more, drawing on the darkness and begging it to give me the strength I needed to get within the king's walls.

Magic exploded from me, going in all directions and

demolishing whatever it touched. The well crumbled before me, the tables nearest to me from the market caught fire, and the mortar between the bricks began to crumble.

Using that much power hadn't been my intention, but it was effective. Several of the guards that had been headed for me stopped, glancing at each other until one of them yelled, "Keep fighting!"

Gabriel still stood back, leaning against the wall with a smirk on his round face. Gods, I couldn't wait to kill him. Spilling his blood would be almost as satisfying as the king's.

Before I could worry about him, I had to contend with those still stupid enough to fight me. The larger group took almost every ounce of energy I had left within me. I took out fae after fae, ignoring every hit they managed to get in when more than two came at me.

By the time I was done with them, I hadn't wavered from my goal. My focus was still on removing whatever obstacles lay in my way of getting inside that castle.

After the last fae went down from the second group, I took stock of my newest injuries. My right wing was back to hanging lower than the left. Blood oozed down my forehead and across my stomach, and I walked with a limp.

Now, there was no one else between me and Gabriel. Even in my tattered state, glee filled me at how close I was to getting my hands on the king.

We will succeed. No matter the cost. We must get to the king, my inner voice encouraged.

"I'm disappointed to say I'm mildly impressed with your fighting skills, Lucinda. It's such a pity I have to kill you now," Gabriel taunted, not at all afraid it was finally just me and him.

"I said not to kill her. She will suffer for taking part in my son's death, and her punishment will be by my hand," King's Zephyr's voice sounded, but he was nowhere to be seen from where I stood.

Find Zephyr. Don't let him hide from us, the voice urged.

As I stepped closer to Gabriel, unafraid of what he might be able to do to me in my weakened state, I glanced through the open gate and caught sight of a struggling blonde behind another dozen guards just inside the king's walls. We weren't so alone after all.

Ivy's fiery gaze met mine, not a single tear in her eye as she nodded. A part of me really wished she didn't have to die, but Neva wasn't back with a witch to save her. If I could get close enough, I wouldn't miss the opportunity to kill the king. Not even for Ivy.

King Zephyr moved his head to the side of hers, but before I could focus on him, Gabriel sent a blast of dark magic toward me, and the power clipped my good wing, bending it into an awkward point.

"Don't play with her, Gabriel. Just capture her and bring her to the dungeon." As I kneeled on the ground, recovering from the most recent blow, I turned back toward the sound of his voice. King Zephyr met my stare and ran his nose through Ivy's blonde locks. "I need Lucinda awake for the first part of her suffering."

Ivy shuddered, then dropped an elbow into his gut. "Keep your damn hands off me."

King Zephyr retaliated with a punch to the back of her head, and Ivy fell to the ground behind the other waiting guards.

Wrath built within me once more. Nobody deserved to be treated like that, especially Ivy. I might have been beaten on the outside, but I wasn't done fighting. The king was the ultimate bully, and I was going to show him what happened when he didn't give others the respect they deserved.

Gabriel took a step toward me as I stood back up. My full focus was on him, wrath bubbling and power continuing to build within my core.

"Are you going to make this fun or disappointing, Lucinda?" Gabriel jeered, and I stumbled to the ground once more, a new plan forming. "Of *course* you're not going to fight. You've always been pathetic. I never could see what the king saw in you. Not even with your unique wings."

The last bit was whispered in my ear as Gabriel grabbed hold of my hair and yanked my head back.

"You know, I normally like rough foreplay, but I'm going to have to pass this time," I snarled, forcing my head forward and into his nose even as his grip tightened around my strands.

The resounding crunch was pleasing, but I knew it wouldn't faze him enough to get me through the gates. I wrapped my hands around his face, sending a wave of magic into Gabriel with enough force to knock him out. Unfortunately, my actions nearly did the same to me.

"Get her!" King Zephyr shouted, and I glanced up in time to see him retreating with Ivy dragging behind him and fighting against his hold.

I took quick stock of my situation and was fully aware of the blood seeping from multiple wounds—mostly from my stomach. My wings were pretty much useless, but I refused to believe any of those things were going to stop me.

I ripped out more feathers and winced when I realized how many I'd grabbed. I'd never utilized my own feathers this much before, but I had to use whatever was at my disposal when magic wasn't enough. The feathers would grow back.

After throwing a handful of sharpened feathers at the advancing horde, I spotted a glowing sword at Gabriel's hip. Crawling toward him since I still couldn't stand, my fingers wrapped around the hilt. The pain caused me to hiss and almost drop it, but my hold tightened against my command as dark magic filled me, allowing me the energy to finally stand again.

End them. Now!

The more magic I soaked in from the blade, the darker my thoughts became. I moved to swing down toward Gabriel and cut his head off, but power burned into my back.

"I love granting death wishes," I stated with a grin as I moved toward the group that had assaulted me. I had no idea who hit me, but the whole lot would pay for their mistake.

Some of them slowed as black magic began to intertwine with my normal teal, but I had to give credit to the six who didn't stop following what had been commanded of them. At least they were loyal, but that wouldn't save them. Nothing would now.

While greedily inhaling the power that the sword was providing, I channeled some of it back through the blade and arced it high in the sky before swinging it around and across the chests of four fae. Their skin burned on contact with the metal, and their knees buckled, but the ones behind them were prepared. The fae I'd thought slowed out of fear were merely preparing.

As more moved forward, three of them stood side-by-side, palms facing me and navy power swirling around their hands. I tried to bring my wings in front of me to use as a shield, but even with the increased adrenaline from the sword, they weren't cooperating.

Before I could think of a plan B, the fae fired off their magic at me all at the same time, and I ended up on my ass as someone called my name from behind.

When I tried to sit up, I realized my hands were empty and the sword was nowhere in my limited sight, causing my energy to wane once more. Another hole was ripped through my bodysuit that should have been nearly impenetrable, and blood soaked through not only at my stomach, but now my shoulder as well.

Everything within me felt broken, but it was my fury that gave me the strength to keep getting up. I wasn't done with these people. I had to get to the king.

A blur of motion flew past me as I crawled to my knees, still failing to stand, but I did lay eyes on the sword. A large part of me was screaming to leave the blade be, but I just needed its power for a little bit longer.

I lifted my head and caught a glimpse of forest-green wings. When my eyes focused, Finn was moving swiftly between the remaining guards knocking those unconscious that he could and even breaking a neck or two on those he couldn't.

I wasn't sure who this new Finn was, but he was glorious and going to be my ticket to the king—him and the sword. I just needed my magic to start healing me and everything would be fine. Finn could get his sister and say goodbye, and I could end the reign of terror that was King Zephyr.

Except, when Finn was done and there were no more guards coming toward us, he didn't do what I expected, what I wanted most.

His gentle hands lifted me up and cradled me to his chest. "Let's go."

Don't let him take you. He will ruin us. Don't let—the inner voice started to yell in my head, but I cut it off, needing to focus.

Finn took a step in the wrong direction, and I fought against his hold. "No. We just killed more than half his personal guard. We need to end this now. It's our best chance."

Adjusting so he could use one hand to grab my chin, he growled in my face. "Lucinda, if I don't get you away from here, you're going to die. You're not healing, and I *have* to save you."

It didn't matter that everything within me was screaming in agony and that he was probably right. I wasn't ready to walk away. I was there to kill the king, and that was what I would do. Or die trying.

"Let me go. I'll be fine. I can use the sword I had." I pushed against his chest, but he didn't seem the least bit deterred from his intentions.

I tried to draw on my darkness, take whatever boost I could get, but something was wrong. The power was just beneath the surface, but it was being smothered. Had I lost too much blood? Was this it for me?

Shit. Maybe I was as bad as he said, but I wasn't ready to give up. If this was where I died, then so be it, but if I was going down, I'd do it fighting.

"You're not going to die. I won't let that happen," Finn grumbled. He tightened his hold on me as the castle disappeared around us and consciousness began to fade away.

CHAPTER 2

*W*hen I came to, I was lying on grass, staring up at a clear blue sky, and listening to the waves crash against the shore. The smell of saltwater was heavy around me. I tried to turn my head, but I couldn't move anything except my eyes.

Closing them, I tried to remember what had happened and where I might be. It wasn't as bad as I last recalled, but I was still in moderate pain, so I was pretty sure I wasn't dead. My ears listened for sounds, and I caught the faint hint of breathing behind me.

I called on my magic, which seemed to be replenished, and let it flow freely from my hands before opening my eyes again.

When I did, Finn's intense silver gaze was peering down on me with emotions I couldn't decipher. "Lucinda."

I blinked, unable to respond and growing more frustrated by the second.

"Are you in control?" he asked, and I wanted to kick him in the balls. He had to know I couldn't actually answer.

I attempted to glare, unsure if it worked until his lips turned into a smirk. "There you are. I'm going to remove the magic binding you, but if you try to go anywhere, Mosi will be back to lock you down again."

Mosi? I really needed to know more about that fae. And, again? Why had he even done it in the first place?

Finn placed one hand on my chest and the other on my forehead. His light fae power flooded through my veins, burning me from the inside out. We might have been two opposites, but instead of trying to move away from the scorching feeling his power ignited within me, my body craved to be closer to it.

When he was done and removed the hand from my head, the other remained on my chest and our eyes locked. Emotions rose to the surface. New emotions that were conflicting as I remembered that he'd taken me away from the fight at the castle that I had so badly wanted to end with the king's death.

Regardless of that, as I took in the charcoal bleeding through his eyes, the darkness that still swelled inside him, and the passion pouring off him in waves, I wanted him more than ever before.

I waited for a snarky comment from my inner voice, but nothing came. It was silent, and not because I was pushing it down.

Wherever my inner darkness had gone, it took away my ability to ignore the attraction I'd always known was between me and Finn. Gods, I wanted him badly, maybe needed him more than ever, but I also didn't at the same time. The inner turmoil was almost enough to make me wish for death as an easy escape.

His hand moved from my chest to my face, fingers stroking my cheek as he leaned in closer. "How are you feeling?" he asked as I sat up.

"You had no right to force me away from that fight," I said instead of answering his question. I wanted to be angry at him, but based on the warmth that was building inside me, I seemed to be breathing heavy for two different reasons.

"You were going to die, and I couldn't let that happen."

My hands gripped his shirt, bringing him closer and trying to remind him why his choice had been wrong for the Finn I thought I knew. "But he has your sister."

"I know, and if he's smart, the king will leave her alive in order to negotiate her life with us. As much as it killed me to leave her behind, I can't save her without you, and you weren't going to make it past the next wave of guards that were headed for us."

I wanted to remind him that even if King Zephyr left Ivy alive, she wouldn't remain unscathed. He could torture her while leaving her in good enough condition to taunt us. Ivy wouldn't be the same sister he once knew if we got her back alive.

All of those thoughts were lost to me, though, as Finn inched closer. I breathed in his heady scent of light magic. It was like warm spring air after the rain. The realization that I'd never wanted someone as much as I wanted him in that moment slammed into me.

There was a small part of me—one that had nothing to do with my inner darkness—that knew I should be questioning my actions, but I was growing tired of fighting all the damn time. I just needed to get Finn Barlow out of my system and then I could worry about what came next. With my wounds mostly healed and the block lifted, I regained control.

I could only think of one thing I wanted most in that moment.

Using my grip still on Finn's shirt, I jerked him close enough to press my lips to his as he cradled the back of my head with his hands. His chest rumbled as I pushed closer and soaked in everything that he was. The goodness inside him that normally repulsed me was suddenly burning a fire within me instead.

I began pulling at his clothes, no longer wanting any layers between us as he did the same to mine, causing me to realize I was no longer in the bodysuit I'd been wearing before. I was covered in a soft white cotton dress—something that seemed so pure and out of place against my skin.

As I continued with frantic movements, Finn paused. His hands wrapped around mine that had been unbuttoning his pants.

"Lucinda, I think—"

I yanked my hand from his grip and pressed it over his mouth. "Finn, we've fought whatever this is for long enough. I almost died, and it would be really great if you didn't make me think too much about that."

He grinned under my hold and gently pulled my fingers back. "That's not where I was going, but I'm glad to know you weren't unaffected before."

Gods, if he only knew, but I'd never admit the feelings he stirred within me out loud.

He resumed pulling the dress over my head as I got his pants unbuttoned.

By the time we were both naked, I was acting on pure passion. I wasn't overthinking what it could mean to have sex with him. I refused to consider the consequences of allowing him in intimately or the reasons my body wanted him so thoroughly in that moment.

With cool grass beneath me, I lay back and let my indigo hair fan out at the sides. I openly appraised everything Finn had on display as he inched closer. Gods, why had I ever fought against the emotions he enticed within me before?

He leaned over me onto his elbows, his muscled arms blocking me in as his thumbs stroked against my outer shoulders. Forcing my eyes from his, I let them wander down his delectable, tanned chest. I lifted a hand, letting my fingers trail down his stomach. Muscles rippled beneath my feather-light touches until my hand wrapped around the silky-smooth skin of his hard length. He growled in response, causing warmth to pool at my center. I was more than ready for him.

Finn shifted his weight, leaning on one arm while the other snaked between us and ended my exploring. With his free hand, he pinned both of mine on the grass behind my head as he sank into me in one fluid motion.

I sucked in a breath as my whole world turned upside down and magic poured from me.

The darkest parts of me finally flared to life again, putting up a feeble fight against what was happening. I'd known there was something different about Finn the moment I saw him, but I'd always assumed it was the dark magic in him that called to me.

This fae will ruin who we've become. Don't let him, the voice sneered.

I should have stopped what was happening. I should have listened, but I didn't. The connection that was forming between Finn and me was more powerful than my stubbornness. Stronger than my hate of feeling emotions that made me vulnerable.

My arms shook as our magic intertwined.

You're going to regret this, Lucinda. Stop it now! the voice shouted, but there was no more power behind its words.

Finn's silver eyes turned to charcoal as my magic hovered above his chest. His grip on me tightened as my shaking slowed.

This is your last chance, the voice growled, yet sounded weaker.

My hands moved to Finn's shoulders. I was going to push him off of me. I was going to stop the bond that was building. My intentions were clear. The voice had finally gotten through my sex-induced haze.

When my nails dug into Finn's skin, he rolled us until I was on top. "I won't force you, but you need to know that I accept you, Lucinda. All of you."

All I had to do was push up onto my feet and there

would be no bond between me and Finn. Just one simple movement and I would keep my freedom. Except I couldn't bring myself to do it. The call of the bond was soothing and powerful. There was a strength within it that calmed my heart in a way I'd never felt before.

Lucinda, no! my inner voice screamed, but it changed nothing for me.

As I locked gazes with Finn, I decided to accept the challenge fate had thrown my way. I might regret it later, but bonds could be broken, and curiosity got the better of me as I let my instincts take over.

Mine, a voice sounded in my mind that wasn't the one I was used to. Instead of fighting against the singular word that held enough power to ruin me, I found myself drawn to it and repeating the same.

Mine, I agreed, and Finn's chest rumbled as we both came together and lay tangled around each other.

Minutes passed before he rose up and stroked my cheek. "I had no idea that we would..."

"Bond? Yeah, bit of a shocker there," I replied, already wondering if I'd made the right choice as the sex fog began to lift.

A commitment like this wasn't something the normal me would be okay with, but there was a euphoria in me that had never been there before, and I couldn't deny it was a nice change.

Comfortable silence settled between us as I pretended that we were just two fae on a beach. Nothing more, nothing less.

"Is this really what you wanted?" he asked hesitantly.

'No' was at the tip of my tongue as I rolled over to face him. I wouldn't lie to Finn. It served no purpose. He knew who I was, and if he'd been telling the truth before about accepting all of me, then he wouldn't appreciate anything less than the truth.

"It wasn't what I wanted, but it happened, and I can see this being a benefit," I said, even if my inner voice had yelled otherwise.

Finn turned toward me with a smile on his face. "Thank you for not lying."

"What about you? You're now tied to me, and I haven't changed, Finn. I'm still going to do whatever it takes to end King Zephyr, and I won't let anyone get in the way of that. Not even what happened today."

My chest constricted at the thought of hurting him, and I wanted to smack myself. Though, I wasn't sure if that was for pretending I couldn't compromise or for caring so much. I knew I had more obstacles in front of me now, but maybe Finn really could understand my side of things with the bond in place. It would sure as hell make me want to punch him less.

He leaned closer to me again, his fingers reaching to play with the ends of my hair. "I've learned to accept you for who you are already. Mosi helped me to see the other side of things. Once I did, he made me promise to keep you alive, no matter the cost. Though, I had no idea *this* would happen if I succeeded."

I moved away from him, sitting up straighter, still naked and uncaring. "What do you mean?"

"Mosi came to me the night before we all went to the castle together. He can see pieces of the future and interferes when he can. He is actually the reason why I went to find you in the first place. During our last meeting, I was so angry with you. Mosi painted things in a way that I could understand your perspective, and the irritation lifted."

"What about keeping me alive?" I asked, more curious how that played into our situation.

"He told me you were our only chance at saving Ivy. I had to choose your life over hers, which was a lot easier to do when I could understand your actions more."

A fae who could see the future? I'd never heard of such a thing, but he also had feathered wings like me. As much as I didn't want to believe it, I knew I couldn't deny the possibility. There was too much unknown about fae like us.

"Tell me everything Mosi said to you before the fight," I demanded as Finn reached for his pants and tossed me the cotton dress. I could have magicked myself some regular clothes, but it was hot as hell under the sun on this island. The dress didn't sound so bad for the time being.

"He said there would be a battle and I'd have to choose between you and Ivy. That in order to save my sister, I'd have to stand by your side and do things I normally wouldn't, like kill other fae without asking questions first."

My mind flashed back first to the battle at the farm and then to the castle when Finn had arrived and began attacking the guards like a madman. Finn's statement might have given some women doubts about his choices, but not me. He'd been up front since the beginning that he needed to save his sister, and I wouldn't hold his actions against him.

"Well, you certainly had no problem acclimating to that. And here I thought it was because I'd rubbed off on you," I said with a grin.

He stood and finished getting dressed. When his face reappeared after his shirt was on, he fought a grin. "I think it was a little of both. Like I said, I didn't choose to accept my feelings after I found out about saving Ivy. I chose you first. Mosi is smart like that."

As I slipped the dress over my head, I knew I couldn't argue with him. The order in which Finn made his choices did help me to believe he wasn't using me only to save his sister.

Finn stepped closer and reached for me. "All of my choices have been mine alone. If you walked away from ending the king and saving Ivy, I still wouldn't regret what happened today. A part of me already knew there was something special about you. I fought against it, because you…" Finn grimaced, unable to find the right words.

"Because I'm me, and who I am goes against everything you believe in. It's okay, Finn. I don't expect us to pretend anything has changed about our views just because fate decided we should be bonded. We are who we are, and you don't have to agree with everything that I am. The bond shouldn't force either of us to be someone different."

Finn gently pushed the wild strands of my hair back behind my ear before speaking. "You were raised by horrid fae, but the things they made you do don't have to dictate who you are. The Lucinda I see now is one who took a screwed-up situation and used it to help other people."

I snorted and glanced at the water in front of us, needing space from his intense gaze. "For a price. I didn't do it out of the kindness of my heart."

He sighed, then softly forced my gaze back to his. "Not always, but the times you did, even if you didn't realize it, count for something."

A power pulsed around us, and I itched to wrap my body around him again. Slowly, the gap between us closed as the air sizzled and I grabbed on to his biceps. "Finn…"

"I know."

The emotions were overpowering. I was drowning in them, and that scared the shit out of me. My heart pounded in my chest as I squeezed tighter and he brought his forehead to mine. "It's going to be okay, Lucy."

I didn't quite believe him but chose to focus on what had happened while I was unconscious instead.

"Where are we, and why was I magically restrained when I woke up?" I asked, glancing around again.

In front of me was only ocean for as far as the eye could see, and behind us was nothing more than a tropical forest. The sun warmed my skin from above, and I inhaled the scent of saltwater once more, this time also sensing magic. Lots of it.

"We're still in the fae realm, but on an island Mosi has had hidden for many years. He brought a witch here that concealed its location. Only supernaturals that Mosi personally allows can enter."

"And why was I restrained?" I asked again since he seemed to be avoiding the question.

He shrugged sheepishly. "Well, your darkness took over the first time you woke up. According to your verbal threats, it wasn't pleased that I'd taken you from the castle and left the sword behind."

"Did I do something besides sling verbal threats?" Hopefully I hadn't killed anyone or done something that would bring us more trouble.

He hesitated again, but I glared hard enough that he finally spoke. "You... No, not you. *It* tried to kill me, but we restrained you before you could do any harm. Do you sense whatever that darkness is now? Mosi's mate tried to help you, but she wasn't sure how well it worked."

I stopped and pulled away from Finn, staring into his eyes that held no blame toward me. He was too good, and that irritated me. Accepting the bond had happened in a heat of passion, but as minutes ticked by, the doubts started to slither in.

"I think it's time I had a better introduction to this mysterious fae that seems to know more about me than I'm comfortable with. Along with his mate," I replied once I had my wits about me again.

He grabbed my hand. "I think they'd like that."

I rolled my eyes. I didn't care if anyone liked it or not. These fae had some explaining to do, and I wasn't leaving this island until they told me a hell of a lot more about whatever was going on. I was beginning to believe there was more at stake than just saving Finn's sister and killing the demons of my past.

Someone was leaving out the details, and I wasn't okay with that.

CHAPTER 3

Instead of teleporting to wherever Mosi was, Finn insisted we walk. I tried to take in our surroundings as we traveled through the trees, but my mind was reeling. Even though I could hear the monkeys, birds, and insects, I could think of nothing other than bonding with Finn.

It was the worst possible scenario. Now that I wasn't in a sex-induced haze, the doubts were nonstop. I could have stopped it. I knew what was happening, and, while all seemed fine in the moment, I was anything but fine.

From what I knew about bonds, we never would have become bonded if we hadn't had sex. The only thing that kept me from really losing my shit was that I knew there was a way to break it. I couldn't remember how it was done. All that mattered was that I was confident it was possible to make the connection go away.

Holy shit, I was bonded.

And not to just any fae. A light one with a strong moral compass. One who not too long ago looked at me with disgust for my actions. Sure, he was beginning to understand me and see my views, but would he expect me to do the same? I knew I should, but could I?

Bonds and emotions made all kinds of people do stupid shit. Neva had been saying I was changing, that I wasn't who I thought I was. Was I becoming someone else just by being around Finn? Having a man dictate my life was my biggest fear after being freed from King Zephyr. Had I somehow just ended up in a similar situation? I'd die before I let Finn control me.

Logically, I knew he was nothing like the king, but Finn now had influence over my actions through the bond. My heart would urge me to make decisions with his interests at the forefront of my choices, but what about my mind? What about the inner me? The inner me who'd been silenced somehow and was no longer able to make me see reason. Well, my version of it anyway.

A new terror rose within me. Even though the voice had become annoying and demanding, it was part of me. The darkness had kept me sane in the early months of being on my own, and I wanted it back.

Finn tugged on my hand. "Are you okay?"

I nodded, afraid my voice would betray me. He wouldn't understand what I was going through. To him, it would be a good thing.

"You do realize it's pointless to lie to your bonded, right?" He was staring down at me, and as I met his gaze, I expected to find contempt, but only concern remained in his eyes.

My heart constricted as I fought against the urge to tell him all my fears. This stupid bond was going to be the death of me.

"I didn't lie. I am okay. My bones are healed. My wings are tucked away, so I assume they're fine. I can walk and breathe. All is good in my world." None of that was false. I'd merely omitted the things that were actually wrong.

He sighed and let the subject go. "We're almost there. Don't forget Mosi's mate Olida helped heal you, so make sure you thank her."

Thank her? For what? Taking away part of me without asking for my opinion. Not a chance in hell. As soon as I got the information out of Mosi, she was going to know exactly what I *wasn't* thankful for.

As my internal freak-out began to wane and I started forming plans in my mind to keep me from losing my cool, I let my gaze wander. There wasn't much to see besides green foliage and tall trees, but I could still hear the animals around us and wondered if they'd been brought in from Earth. The main islands didn't have too many animals outside of the ones that could help work the farms and birds that somehow found their way through the portal from Earth to Fae Islands on occasion.

The forest began to thin, and structures started to appear. Small huts, made from bamboo and palm leaves, were lifted off the ground about a foot. Most of them appeared to be one room structures from the outside, but the further we walked, the bigger they became until one in the center caught my attention.

The wooden door creaked open, and a woman stepped out. Her dark hair hung to her waist and was braided with silver streaks running through it. Her ebony skin was the darkest I'd ever seen, but it didn't hold my attention for long as our eyes met. Hers were light purple and glowed under the afternoon sun. As she smiled at me, wrinkles formed, and any unease I'd been feeling disappeared.

She waltzed toward me with arms open, magic pouring off her in waves. "Lucinda! It's lovely to see you walking. I think you topped my list of hardest healing jobs."

I stepped back as she inched closer, but the woman seemed to know my next move before I did, and I found myself in her embrace anyway. I struggled to get away first, intent to give her a piece of my mind about her *healing*, but her hold on me strengthened and my resistance softened as her magic permeated around us.

My muscles relaxed, and I stopped fighting against her without meaning to. "You've healed nicely, child," the woman murmured in my ear. She squeezed once more, and energy tingled along my exposed skin. "This makes me happy," she added as she backed up.

"Olida, my love. Give the girl some space. She doesn't know who we are." Mosi appeared through the same door, grinning as he walked toward us.

He and Finn clasped forearms and half hugged before the unknown fae turned his attention on me. "Lucinda, I'm sorry our previous introduction was cut short, but I can't be exposed yet. I never would have left you to fight Zephyr on your own otherwise."

"Well, I'd love to know more about why that is and what the hell has been happening, because clearly nothing is as it seems around here." I fought to keep the snark out of my tone considering they'd saved my life and had information I needed.

Mosi reached for me, grasping my elbow. "Yes, that is correct. Let's go inside. We have tea and food waiting for you. There is much to celebrate and discuss."

I snorted. Celebrate? He was out of his damn mind. "King Zephyr is still alive. There is nothing to celebrate until he's nothing more than a bad memory."

Mosi's mahogany eyes glowered at me, and he dropped his hold as his hands turned to fists. "That fae is no king, and we do not address him as such on this island." Then, he turned abruptly to go back inside the hut with Olida right behind him.

Finn smiled softly at me and shrugged. "Mosi is very passionate about his purpose in this life. Just go with it."

Right. Like that would be easy for me to do.

When we entered the hut, it was even bigger than I expected, mostly taller. The first level was an open living area with wood-planked floors, a fireplace, large pillows for the only seats, and a small kitchen where Olida was already gathering items.

Finn guided me toward the cushions, and we both sat, following Mosi's lead. Olida set a tray of fruit in the middle and took her place beside her mate, holding his hand. They shared an intense gaze, and I nearly choked on the strawberry I'd grabbed. Emotions slammed into me, and Finn patted my back.

Even without my inner voice, I clearly still had problems with public displays of affection, but it was different than before. This time, there was a bit of jealousy there and *that* was something I'd never experienced.

I knew nothing about mates. I barely knew anything about Finn. I had no idea how all of this was supposed to work, and I didn't like all of the uncertainties, but at least our chemistry had always been hot. Everything else, though, put me on edge as I waited for Mosi to start explaining what the hell was going on.

"Where shall we start?" Mosi asked, grabbing his tea and taking a sip.

"How about the beginning? Why did you send Finn to find me?" I asked.

Mosi grinned above his cup. "Oh, child. That's not the beginning. Everything that is happening around you started many years ago. Zephyr has been after you since the day you were born."

"What?" Finn snarled while I sat there in shock. Though, I was thankful that he hadn't known that detail. If he'd been keeping anything big to do with my past from me, I wasn't sure I'd be able to forgive him. Hiding his relationship with Mosi was one thing, but anything more was crossing a line I couldn't come back from. Bond or no bond, I would hurt him.

"What do you mean he's been after me?" I asked.

"Well, when you were born and you exposed feathered wings, your parents didn't know what to do with you. All they'd known was that fae like you were an abomination. So, they'd gone to see the queen, but Zephyr found them first."

Abomination. That was certainly one word for how they'd made me feel.

Mosi continued, "Zephyr convinced them you were perfect as is, that there was nothing wicked about you. He promised them that if you did anything wrong, he would take full responsibility for it."

My hands tightened around the cup I held. "Of course, they were only concerned I'd ruin their standing. All they ever cared about was moving up the social ladder."

Mosi held my gaze. "Unfortunately, that is true. With Zephyr's interest in you, they went along with whatever he said. Your parents didn't have an easy upbringing of their own. While that doesn't justify their actions, if you knew, it might help things make more sense."

I narrowed my eyes at him, slamming the cup I'd been holding down so hard that liquid spilled onto the floor. "I don't give a damn about the people who gave me life. They were never parents to me, and I hope to never see them again."

Olida stiffened next to Mosi, and he held her hand, but she kept her head high as her gaze intensified on me. "Your parents were killed after they tried to blackmail Zephyr. They were demanding money from him after they saw what he was using you for. Zephyr doesn't take kindly to threats, and Gabriel took care of them."

She paused, seeming to be waiting for a reaction out of me. I could feel Finn staring at me, but I wasn't sure what any of them expected. I would not cry for either of the people who created me. I meant what I said, and this new information was nothing more than peace of mind. My parents had brought whatever fate they were served onto themselves. They could have loved me, but they'd chosen not to. Everything after that was on them.

Trying to get the conversation back on track, I asked, "Why did Zephyr have such an interest in me? I'm not the first fae born with feathered wings."

Mosi nodded. "That is true, but you are the first who couldn't be classified as either a light or dark fae."

No. No, that couldn't be right. My vision blurred as I tried to understand what he was saying. I'd always known who I was and what I was. Mosi had to be wrong.

"What the hell did you just say?"

CHAPTER 4

Magic pulsed off me in sync with the pounding of my heart. Mosi had to be mistaken. There was no way that could be true. I was filled only with a powerful darkness. It had guided me my whole life. Maybe this fae wasn't as wise as he'd convinced Finn.

"I know this is hard to understand, but it is true. I've met plenty of our kind, and it's usually a similar story, but yours is the most unique I've found. The other feathered fae, me included, have both light and dark magic within them, but we can't choose between the two. Though, what's surprised me the most during all of this is how Finn has become like the rest of us."

Finn glanced at me and then back at Mosi, his ire also rising. "What does *that* mean?"

I wasn't going to make it much longer before I really lost my shit and any chance of getting answers. Mosi was making it really hard for me to see reason, given the words coming out of his mouth.

Olida stood. "Dear, you better move that mouth of yours faster, or these two will leave us. I'm going to get something stronger than this tea, and you better be done when I'm back."

Now *that* was the kind of fae I could possibly like. Though, for her, it was still to be determined given she'd screwed with my head.

Mosi watched his mate leave the hut with a shimmer of something in his eyes I didn't understand, but suddenly, I wanted to. *Damn bond.*

"My better half is right. Please, have patience with me. It will make sense when I am done," he said.

"Talk fast," was my only reply.

Mosi nodded. "Lucinda, when you were born to dark fae parents, it made sense for you to be dark as well. When you didn't associate one way or the other, Zephyr made it seem as if you were dark by using magic of his own to avoid any questions from anyone who might encounter you. Fae don't know much about our feathered kind, so there was never any reason to doubt you couldn't be a welcomed part of our community."

I scoffed. "Welcomed" was a bit farfetched.

Mosi nodded at me. "I've already mentioned how you ended up in the care of Zephyr. He turned you into the weapon he always hoped you'd be, but just like everything else in his life, when you began to find your own sense of understanding, he thought you were worthless."

I cut him off. "But why me? Why did he choose me at all?"

"While everyday fae aren't familiar with the feathered fae, the royalty always has been. We all have a special trait that makes us sought after. Hence, why you don't normally find them in the fae realm. There are too many selfish people in this world for our kind to assimilate themselves normally.

"Now, this part I can only assume, but it's likely Zephyr wanted to groom you into his weapon in hopes your special ability would be worth the trouble of raising you as his own. After a while, you showed no extraordinary talents and were growing a conscience. He used that shifter as a way to get rid of you without looking like the bad guy."

Just when my fury was beginning to settle, it was once again on the rise. "You're telling me that Zephyr set me up to murder an innocent shifter that he'd already tortured for much too long?"

"I'm afraid so."

"Why? None of this makes sense," I seethed.

"Lucinda, you won't ever understand why, because you are not him. You are not consumed with the longing for more power. While some of the fae are aware he's vile, most are not. Zephyr couldn't have thrown a young fae out of the castle without just cause. You killing the shifter that people thought he took care of was reason enough. With one strike, two problems were taken care of for him."

Regret for not stepping up earlier plowed into me. How could I have been so stupid for so long? I should have killed King Zephyr the moment he began forcing me to hurt innocent people. I had known better, and yet, I'd done nothing but follow his blind orders. When I really thought about it, I was just as bad as the king.

Mosi leaned forward and took my hand. "You had no choice. The things you did kept you alive. None of this is your fault. Zephyr is the only one to blame here, and you will make him pay."

"It would have been better if he'd just killed me," I spat.

I wasn't sure if it was the bond or something else, but I was tired. Tired of all the lies and tricks and whatever else. I had always been proud of my strength, always loved who I was, but this was a lot, even for someone like me who fought so hard not to give a shit about anything.

Finn jerked me from Mosi's grasp, his hands cupping my cheeks. "Don't you ever say that again."

Wherever our skin touched, I could sense the magic of the bond flaring to life. Finn's silver eyes bore into me while emotions I could identify but didn't understand filtered from him to me.

"This world is not better with you dead. Don't let Zephyr win," Finn added before releasing my face and moving closer until our shoulders and sides were touching. "Please continue, Mosi."

"Once you were gone, Lucinda, the king was desperate for more power. He had spent the last five years believing you would be the key to his success, yet he had nothing to show for it. Coincidentally, the Renegades had a trap set for him that aligned perfectly with the situation. They'd lured Zephyr with a powerful spell, and it would have killed him if not for Ivy."

Finn tensed beside me, and it was my turn to offer him comfort—something I couldn't recall ever doing for anyone before, but somehow felt natural with Finn as my fingers intertwined with his. The bond was stronger than I expected it to be and continued to frighten the hell out of me.

Doing things like this was not me, but I couldn't seem to stop the actions.

"Is Ivy going to die?" Finn asked.

Mosi frowned. "I cannot answer that question. Not because I won't, but because there are many possible futures. We each have choices to make, and every one can result in a different outcome for us all, but I will do my best to help you get her back if that remains my path."

Finn grimaced, clearly not happy with that answer, but gestured for Mosi to continue anyway.

"Ivy taking on the darkness was a key role in what is happening now. I know watching her suffer is hard. I wish it didn't need to be the way it is, but everything is happening for a reason. Finn, if you hadn't taken on the dark magic within Ivy, you never would have been able to bond with Lucinda."

"What do you mean?" I asked before he could.

I knew very little about bonded mates. Really just two things. That it only happened if you had sex and that it could be broken with powerful—and more importantly, painful—magic. Considering it had never been a path I saw for me, I'd never concerned myself with learning more.

"Light fae cannot bond to dark fae, and vice versa. Even though you were neither light nor dark, Lucinda, you'd been doused in enough darkness that you became a dark fae. Your very essence recognizes that, but you can also change it. You could be light fae if you wanted, or you could be neither."

I stared blankly at him. I didn't really know how to respond to that statement. After everything he'd already said and allowing the bonding to happen, I felt like I'd been kicked from the finish line all the way back to the beginning. I was going to have to figure out what I wanted all over again and I wasn't happy about that, but I couldn't deny that I was also intrigued about some of it.

"Are you saying I could no longer be fae?" I asked.

"No, that's not exactly right, but if what I know is correct, you could cease to use your magic and eventually you would age faster. Your life would be much shorter than that of a typical fae, but still longer than a human's."

I stared blankly at him, having not expected that kind of answer. Giving up magic wasn't natural. It shouldn't be possible. Even if the scenario was plausible, I didn't think it was something I was capable of.

Mosi continued when I didn't reply, "Like I was saying before, though. In order to bond together, Finn had to have the same essence within him. Given that the darkness he took from Ivy came from Zephyr, it worked out just the way I had hoped. That was when I was able to step in and offer Finn my guidance."

"You knew Ivy was going to be poisoned and you did nothing to stop it?" Finn snarled from beside me.

"Calm, young Finn. Everyone has their path, and this was Ivy's. She could have denied Zephyr, and we'd be having a very different conversation right now. I didn't know for sure what would happen, but even if I did, I won't ever interfere with destiny. Even when I don't agree with it," Mosi said with complete confidence.

Just as Finn began to disagree, Olida returned. She held a basket in one hand and used the other to cover her chest. "Mosi, what have you done to these children? You're not making them feel any better. This room is filled with darkness and hostility."

She put the basket down and went around the room lighting bundles of herbs I wasn't familiar with. The scent was heady yet calming in a way I wouldn't have expected. I took several more deep breaths before she handed me and Finn each a cup of something warm.

"What is this?" Finn asked.

Olida grinned as she sat down. "A hot toddy. Made from the finest whiskey those humans on Earth are capable of producing. I make Mosi bring me as many barrels as he can every time he visits."

The first taste exploded on my tongue as I tried to capture all of the flavors: whiskey, honey, a little bit of lemon, and a heavy dose of spice.

"Damn, Olida. I really wanted to not like you, but

you're making it rather hard," I said after my third gulp.

She beamed, wrinkles forming around her unnatural lavender eyes. "I'm going to take that as a compliment. Now, let's get back to it. Where did my mate leave off? I'm sure I can finish it from there and make this less painful."

I had so much happening in my life that I didn't agree with. So much that I thought I needed to be leery of that I decided in that instant, regardless of her past choices, Olida and I were going to be friends. She emitted a powerful aura even *I* couldn't ignore. There was something soothing about her. After the shitshow that had been happening, I wasn't going to deny that I needed more of a calming effect in my life.

Finn set his now-empty cup down. "He just finished telling us how he did nothing to save my sister when he knew what was happening."

Olida glared at Mosi and waved her hand. "You're fired from storytelling. Finn, your sister is going to be okay. Don't you worry about that. She is strong. I have seen it myself. Now, what is really important here, is that all of those past choices made it possible for the two of you to find each other. Can we accept that and move on?"

I shrugged and glanced at Finn. I wasn't the one upset. Olida was right. Ivy was stronger than I think Finn had ever given her credit for, and she'd acknowledged her fate long before I showed up. Finn just had to accept it as well.

One of the ways I'd been able to move on so easily

after I'd been banished from the fae realm was because I took the worst of those memories and moved on. I didn't dwell on them. Tucking them far into the recesses of my mind helped me to become the person I was today.

Although, I wasn't completely oblivious to how not dealing with those things was biting me in the ass now.

When neither of us responded to Olida's question, she repeated herself. "We will move on, correct?"

"Sure. Whatever," Finn muttered.

Or he could just pretend to agree and stew about it by himself. That worked, too.

Olida didn't seem deterred by his flippant comment and carried on. "So, Lucinda. You have a magic within you that was placed at birth and again when you were ten. From what I could tell when I healed you, that voice you no longer hear inside your head was from that magic. I believe Zephyr placed it there in hopes of using it to control you, but little did he know, you're stronger than that."

My jaw tensed as I considered her words. I wanted to tell her she was wrong. The voice had been a vital part of me. It was my own conscience taking on a more powerful role. There was no way it could have been fabricated. But then, I thought about everything Zephyr had done, all that he was capable of, and I couldn't deny the plausibility of her statement.

When I didn't respond, she continued, "When Finn showed up, the natural bond between the two of you began to form and threatened the power within you. Again, just going off speculation, I assume the voice you heard had already begun trying to guide you in certain directions. As you got stronger by being near Finn, the dark magic became more desperate. Did you sense that happening before you lost control after the fight at the castle?"

As I met her gaze, it was as if she could see into my soul. I didn't like that one damn bit. I opened my mouth to lie to her, and she smirked, giving her head the slightest shake.

I turned toward Finn. "Where the hell did you find these people?"

He shrugged. "They found me."

As much as I liked her no-nonsense attitude, I wasn't telling her anything else. Olida could roll with her "speculations" and I'd just keep listening. For now.

"I will take your non-answer as answer enough. Well, now that you've bonded with Finn, the foreign magic within you has been destroyed. You are, for the first time in your existence, completely in control of yourself," Olida said, leaning back and still grinning.

Gods, she reminded me of myself and Neva put together. It was annoying and intriguing all at the same time.

I pointed a finger at Olida then Mosi. "You two are something else. I'm not sure what, or if I even care to figure it out, but regardless, thanks for the story time. Now, while I decide if any of it makes a difference to me, why don't you tell me how it all factors into destroying Zephyr?"

Mosi sighed, glancing at his mate. "She's going to be even more stubborn than we foresaw, isn't she?"

Olida patted his knee. "Not stubborn, dear. Strong. Magnificent. Resilient."

A part of me still wanted to dislike Olida, but the fae was making it damn hard. I'd never had anyone look at me with such hope. Though, I wasn't going to take that wistfulness and pretend it didn't mean they might be using me for their own benefit. I'd be nice to both of them, but my guard would remain up.

Finn refilled my cup, then his own, with more hot toddy. "So, what now? When do we head back to the castle? I won't leave my sister there forever. My patience will only last for so long."

"I understand, and I appreciate your trust in me with my plans. I promise it will not be for nothing. Our time to face Zephyr is coming soon. First, you must find Maddox, and Neva needs to come back."

Maddox. I'd completely forgotten about him and probably owed him an apology, even if he didn't realize it.

"Is he even alive?" I asked, and Finn flinched beside me.

Mosi nodded. "Yes, but he won't be for much longer if the two of you don't act at just the right time. You will find him on his farm, but be wary. Not all of the Renegades were captured by my people, and the guards still hunt for the both of you. We won't know for some time who is truly on our side."

My wings twitched under my shoulder blades at the thought of the guards. I pictured Gabriel's face and the shame for not slicing his head off when I had the chance rolled through me, causing a shudder.

"We find Maddox, get Neva back here, and then we can save my sister and kill the king?" Finn pressed, still hoping for confirmation.

Mosi sighed. "I cannot say for certain, but that is my hope. The future is not as sound as one would hope. I will keep watching and guiding as best I can, but my gift is not without its faults."

Finn grimaced beside me while I finished the warm whiskey. Once I set my cup back down, I decided I was done with this meeting. "Well, I need some air. How far are we from North Island?"

"A day's flight. We are at the furthest point from the castle. You will need to teleport to Finn's farm, but not just anywhere. Only certain spots are safe," Mosi answered.

"While the rest of you figure out the details of our next move, I'm going to stretch my wings. And don't take too long, or I'll leave without you and deal with whatever risks come my way." I winked at Finn when he glowered at me.

I wouldn't really leave without him—we were in this together at this point. But I would go without Mosi's permission if I felt it was right.

I might not fully accept the bond with Finn, but I wasn't stupid. I'd heard Olida, and I did feel stronger without that incessant voice inside my head. Whether I liked it or not, I was beginning to see that maybe bonding hadn't been the end of the world for me.

My stubbornness was bad enough that I wouldn't admit it to him. I would still be me, and Finn would either be okay with that or not. I likely wasn't going to make it easy on him, either. I needed to know that nothing could make him regret being bound to me. That he would be in this no matter who I was or what my beliefs were.

If I could be certain of that, then maybe everything would work out, but I wasn't holding my breath just yet.

CHAPTER 5

*W*hen I exited the hut, my head spun a little. There must have been more whiskey than anything else in those hot toddies, which made me appreciate Olida even more. Sneaky fae.

Once I had my bearings, I looked up to find five fae staring at me. I held my head high as I glared at each one of them. That was, until each of them bowed their head and placed a fist over their chest in respect.

The eldest male stepped forward. "We are glad to see you are safe, Lucinda Morrow. Please accept this gift."

His arms stretched forward with palms up. Within his hands was a feather carved from wood and possibly colored with charcoal. I gently picked it up, the tip sharp, much like my own feathers when I wanted them to be.

"Why?" I asked while marveling at the craftsmanship of the object.

"Because we believe in Mosi, and he believes in you.

We will fight with you when the time comes." He lifted his head just enough so that his azure eyes met mine. I saw nothing in them but sincerity.

"Thank you," I said in earnest, my gaze moving back to the feather I spun within my fingers.

By the time I glanced back up, the five of them were gone and nobody else was around. I had no idea how many fae lived on this island or what they did all day, but I was suddenly okay with being here.

There were very few times in my life when someone looked at me with respect. More often than not, fear and disgust were thrown my way. I'd pretended not to care for a long time, but without the voice inside me, I was beginning to worry I wouldn't be the same confident fae I'd always portrayed.

Unease settled in me as I spread my wings and pushed into the sky. Considering the island was supposed to be a fortress and hidden from anyone who didn't belong, I took my time soaring around the island, trying to leave my worries behind.

The huts below me disappeared under the treetops of the jungle, and I flew high in the air until I sensed the barrier. A warmth coated my skin, almost as if cautioning me from proceeding. When I was as far up as I was going to get, I hovered in the clear blue sky.

The island was a small oval shape, and the jungle-forest took up three-quarters of it. Beyond the trees was a sandy beach, continuing all the way around. I flew across the land, searching for more fae, but not finding any through the thick covering of branches.

When I was done stretching my wings, I drifted

down to the shore and settled on a fallen log. The waves were calm, and the birds were plentiful. Their songs kept most of my thoughts at bay, but only for a short time.

Mosi had revealed more than I expected. My entire life wasn't what I thought it was. *I* wasn't who I thought I was, yet I was certain I didn't want to change. Most of it didn't make sense just yet. I had a feeling it wouldn't for some time.

On top of all that, I was mated to Finn.

"Mated."

Saying the word out loud made my skin shiver along my spine and down my arms. Though, I couldn't decide if it was in fear or disgust of the emotions I couldn't comprehend.

Neva had been the only person to show me some semblance of friendship, and I'd never truly accepted it. I'd always fought against letting her get close, because if I cared too much, that gave her the power to destroy me. Even if it wasn't her intention.

Now, I had Finn and this bond between us. Something very permanent and not easy to avoid. Even as I sat staring into the waters of the fae realm, I could sense him when I searched. I instinctively knew he was safe, but I couldn't tell what he was doing in that exact moment.

"Gods, this isn't me," I muttered to myself.

"Are you sure about that?" Olida's voice sounded right before she took a seat next to me.

My body flinched, but I held back my natural

reaction to strike out. "It's rude to eavesdrop on people."

"Well, I didn't expect you to be talking to yourself," she countered. "I've been around for a couple centuries, Lucinda. I've seen all kinds of people, watched the worlds change, and had my fair share of hurt, but never before have I sensed what I do in you."

I side-eyed her. "And what would that be?"

"Exactly what I told Mosi earlier—strength, magnificence, and resilience." Her wrinkled hand grabbed on to mine as she sat down. "You have suffered much in your short life. You are still just a child in my eyes, but you have the mind of someone far beyond your physical years. But don't hate the path you have taken. Everything that you are is what will get you through the trying times to come."

I laughed. "I think you're the first, and only, person to ever think that way about me."

"No, I'm just the first person you've believed. The important question is why is it that you've failed to accept these things about yourself before? You know you're powerful. You know you can handle plenty on your own. Why can't you see your own self-worth?"

Olida wasn't pulling any punches, and I didn't like it. I'd come out here for air and to get away from the heavy, but she wasn't letting that happen.

"A part of why you trust me is because there is no longer a darkness within you that is telling you not to. I'm sure you might miss its companionship. You were alone for so long. But remember, you have that with

Finn now. You don't ever have to be on your own again. Finn accepts you for who you are."

A splash in the water caught my attention, and I used it as a distraction to avoid responding. Not having the darkness within me wasn't going to change all of my thoughts and views on life. I still didn't believe Finn could truly accept me for who I was. He might have gone along with what Mosi said, but that very well could have been to save his sister, even if he'd said otherwise.

"What are you?" I asked, needing a change in subject.

"I'm assuming you mean besides the obvious." I nodded, and she continued. "Well, even that I'm not really sure of. You see, the two of us, we're a lot alike. There is much unknown about me, as there is you. I can heal people, but it doesn't always work the same way every time. I can sense emotions, and even sometimes relieve the pain of the past. But each time I use my abilities, it's always a little different."

"At least you're a light fae. People don't fear the unknown when it comes from fae like you," I replied, my voice drenched in bitterness. We weren't alike. She had no idea about the life I'd lived.

She tsked. "That's where you're wrong. I was nearly killed for my abilities only a century ago. That's when Mosi found me. He saved my life and brought me here. I haven't left since."

"The world is different now. Your kind of powers would be sought after and praised," I said.

"Fear makes people do crazy things, Lucinda. What

astounds me about you, and even makes me a little jealous, is that you don't let your fears keep you from doing what you want. That is something you should be proud of."

I nodded, taking in her words as we both stared out into the waves until the sun began to set. The rays cast shades of orange and red onto the water, and when they'd nearly disappeared, Olida stood.

"I'm going to leave you be now. You know where I am if you decide you want to talk more, and I hope you'll remember that you're not on your own anymore." Olida's gossamer wings spread, reflecting off the setting sun with a rainbow of colors.

Deciding it was likely time to head back myself so we could find Maddox, I extended my own wings and followed her to the main area of the island. When we landed outside their house, I waited several feet beyond the door as she headed inside the hut.

I was missing my apartment badly. I needed my own space to escape to, and it had been two weeks since that existed. Two weeks too long.

Finn stepped out of the hut just moments after Olida entered. When our eyes met, his shimmered with passion and I wondered—not for the first time—what he saw when he looked at me. Was it different than before? Could he really forget the contempt he'd felt for me just days earlier? His eyes said yes, but my thoughts believed otherwise.

I also wondered, if I asked myself the same questions, would I be okay with the responses? It was a lot to worry about from both sides. I'd felt like a war was raging within me ever since I woke up on the beach, but that was a problem to deal with later.

"Mosi gave us a place to stay while we're here. Come on." Finn reached out a hand to me.

When I hesitated to take it, he sighed and stepped forward to hold on to me anyway. It made me smile that he took charge.

He led us down a dirt path between the huts and further into the dense jungle. We walked for several minutes until trees began to thin once again and a singular hut came into view. Finn held his hand out, gesturing for me to go first.

I pushed open the wooden door, tensing slightly as the hinges creaked. Stepping inside, I wasn't sure what to expect, but it sure as hell wasn't a large bed, dresser with a mirror above it, and small kitchen area. It was smaller than Mosi and Olida's place, but just as nice. The walls were made from the same bamboo and when I inhaled, all I got was stale air.

"Nobody has used this place for a while," I stated, moving toward a hanging curtain to find a shower, small sink, and toilet which was really just a wooden box set over a hole in the ground with a seat on top of it. The only plus was there were no smells coming from it, probably thanks to magic, and I couldn't see the bottom of the pit below.

Finn hummed as he took it in as well. "Mosi said our best chance at finding Maddox was going to be in the daylight. Since it isn't safe to sleep at my farm, he also suggested we stay here for the night, then leave an hour before sunlight. Hopefully, it won't take us long to find Maddox. Then, we can get Neva and head back here by the end of tomorrow."

I grinned. Neva would love this place. She'd enjoy Olida as well. Though, I didn't miss the urgency in Finn's voice. He was eager to get these tasks done with and head to the castle. The worry for Ivy didn't seem far from his thoughts, and while I didn't understand the kind of bond they shared as brother and sister, I was beginning to accept the importance of it.

My eyes landed on the bed. The comforter was white and covered with several pillows. My body relaxed at just the sight of them. Finn was suddenly much closer than I expected him to be, and my pulse increased. His hand cupped my elbow as he pulled me against his hardened body.

"Lucinda."

"Finn."

"We should probably talk about what happened earlier a little more now that you've had some time to think about it," he said.

"I don't really have anything to say."

That made him grin. "Your eyes tell me otherwise, so why don't you be honest? You didn't have a problem with doing so before."

He was right about that. I shouldn't have qualms about telling him I wasn't sure I wanted to keep the bond. My racing heart had a way of keeping my mouth shut, afraid I wouldn't like what I had to say.

There was a difference between being honest about what I thought and what I felt. One was a hell of a lot scarier.

He held me tighter. "Don't shut me out, Lucy. Say your piece."

I tilted my head up, enjoying the glint of the light that casted off the stubble on his jaw from the lantern in the corner. I missed the twitch that used to appear when I frustrated him. His eyes didn't leave mine, the middle of them still silver but the outer ring darker than ever before.

"I won't change who I am for you," I stated.

"I would never ask you to."

"I don't trust that you actually like me. You are all in with the fae world. The bond is telling you that I'm made for you, but do you really feel that way? Attraction is one thing, but liking who I am is a whole different story. You hated me just mere days ago," I added, disliking that I felt exposed by saying so.

Both of his hands moved to my face, cradling me gently as if I was the most precious thing in all the worlds to him. "Lucinda, listen to me. I will tell you this as many times as I need to, but I'd rather you believe it the first time. I never hated you."

I raised a brow at him. That was a lie, and he knew it.

"Okay, I hated who I thought you were. Neva was right. I don't believe you've ever been the soulless villain I saw burning farms all those years ago. The one who made me wonder if mine would be next. Those past feelings have nothing to do with the Lucinda I see before my eyes. The one I tried so hard to deny but couldn't. Even without being bonded. I had no idea about the bond when I kissed you in that castle."

His lips were only a breath away from me now. The intensity of his gaze and the deep baritone of his voice made my heart race wildly.

"I tried to hate you, because I knew you were right about so many things, but I wasn't strong enough to do the things you had no problem taking care of. I couldn't allow myself to admit I'd been wrong, and that was my biggest mistake."

I couldn't breathe right. Emotions clogged my throat. Speaking wasn't something I was capable of. I didn't know how to respond to Finn, but he seemed to understand that. Words weren't necessary any longer when desires were so heightened by his confessions.

He kissed me softly. Our bodies aligned perfectly, and I found myself practically crawling onto him. Any doubts I'd had before were long gone as our bond flared to life, and this morning's sex was not enough to satisfy me any longer.

With the pull of the bond urging me forward, I hated the little doubts that filtered in. The old me whose thoughts weren't gone, but also weren't loud enough to stop me from wanting what was now mine.

Finn was my mate. The confirmation caused a warmth in my stomach that spread north and south. I wanted him. Badly. Even if I couldn't be his mate forever, I was going to enjoy the benefits of the bond for at least a little while.

Neither of us knew what tomorrow would bring. The tension in my chest loosened as I pressed myself against Finn, accepting the importance of letting him comfort me and wash away the doubts for the time being.

I wasn't naïve enough to think sex would fix everything I'd been worried about earlier, but it was one hell of a way to start.

CHAPTER 6

We stayed in the hut for the rest of the night, spending hours getting to know each other for the first time without any kind of hostility. It wasn't the kind of thing I'd normally do, but the bond was forcing me to consider Finn's wants, and he seemed to need the conversation time as well as the sexual bits.

Finn had a heart much too pure for the world I normally lived in, but there was also an underlying sense of resentment toward the life he'd been living. To Finn, he'd done everything right, been the perfect son and brother. But, no matter how he tried to keep to the values his parents taught him, everything kept falling apart around him, beginning with their death nearly three years ago.

Just as I finished recreating and putting on my favorite jeans and shirt, Finn came back inside the hut carrying food, seeming a lot lighter than he had been the night before.

My stomach growled as the smells hit me. I couldn't remember the last time I'd had a proper meal, so I was drooling over the fresh bread and salads he held.

"Compliments of Olida." Finn hadn't even set the tray down before I was grabbing a bowl and sitting on the bed.

Without saying a word to him, I devoured as much food as I could until I was groaning. "I hate to say it, but I think I love her."

"Olida? I've only met her once before. Mosi usually came to me, and she never leaves the island," Finn replied.

"Yeah, she told me about that yesterday. I couldn't do it. Stay in the same place for decades."

He inched closer, taking my empty dish and putting it on the dresser. "What else did the two of you talk about?"

I winked at him, pushing away to stand. "Wouldn't you like to know. Come on. It's time to go."

The sun hadn't risen, and we'd gotten no sleep, but I was still energized from whatever stasis I'd been in while I was healing from the battles the day before.

"How long was I asleep after you brought me here?" I asked after realizing I'd never questioned how much time had passed.

"About thirty-six hours. Why?"

"It's been two days since we left the castle?" Gods, poor Ivy. I might not have felt bad that she might die in order for me to kill Zephyr, but to be tortured as I imagined she was… it wasn't right. She was better off dead.

After Finn nodded in confirmation, I headed toward the door before remembering this entire island was shielded. "Can we teleport out of here?"

"Yeah, Mosi marked us with his magic so that we could come and go whenever we needed. You can consider this a safe haven for as long as we need it. Nobody will break through these barriers unless Mosi wants them to," Finn replied.

The darkness within me and its voice may have disappeared, but the negative thoughts didn't. I instantly was on guard that Mosi had "marked" us. What did that mean exactly? Could he track us? Force us to do things we didn't want? Magic in older fae like him could be dangerous in the wrong hands. I wanted to trust Mosi, but knowing I hadn't been asked first didn't sit well with me.

Never mind that I was likely halfway to death when he'd done it.

Ignoring that bit of information for the time being, I knew we had to do two things before I could resume my vengeance on the king: find Maddox and get Neva back from Earth.

"Maddox's farm first?" I asked once we were both outside the hut.

"Yeah. I have a feeling any trouble we might find will be waiting for us at mine. I'd rather not have to find him while we're fighting off guards."

"Or killing them," I muttered under my breath while I spread my wings. Either Finn didn't hear me or pretended not to.

His wings extended as he grabbed my hand,

sending a wave of magic through me at the contact. Tiny pinpricks of magic skittered along my skin, something that happened every time we touched but became more natural with each occurrence.

When we adjusted to the bond once again, Finn teleported us to Maddox's farm. I'd never actually been there and had no clue where we were going. As we reappeared, I opened my mouth to ask a question, but the words were lost when the destruction around us practically smacked me in the face.

My hand covered my nose as the smell of sulfur and lingering smoke permeated my senses, making me gag. What had Zephyr been thinking? He was going to ruin his own kingdom. There would be nothing left for him to rule at this rate.

Maddox had mostly crops on his farm and a smaller section of trees around the perimeter, but I only knew that from the scorched branches and the dirt areas I could see from where we stood. Everything, including the house, was flattened.

"If he's still here, Finn…" I didn't want to state the obvious, but things weren't looking good for Maddox.

"Mosi said we had to get him. That means he should still be alive," Finn said, voice tight with anger.

He began walking, and I gingerly followed behind, watching every place I stepped. I had no idea if any fae had died here, possibly burned alive, and I had no desire to step on their bones. Hell, if there was anything left. My feet were warming from the still-sizzling ground, telling me that the flames had burned extraordinarily hot and there was a solid chance we wouldn't find proof of anything by the time we were done.

Glancing around, there was nowhere for anyone to hide, but even still, I sent a wave of magic out just to be sure there was nothing to sense around us.

Finn seemed to know exactly where he was going, trudging along as he cast glances at certain areas, only pausing twice before we arrived at a boulder half a mile from where we started.

He pressed his hand to the rock, power pouring from him, and I was slammed in the chest with remorse —not mine, but Finn's. Seeing this was hurting him more than I realized, but I had no idea what I was supposed to do about it. Did I hug him and tell him everything was going to be okay? No, I couldn't do that. It would be a lie.

Things were going to get much worse.

Instead, I told myself it was best to stand behind him, waiting for him to tell me what he needed. Well, that was only until several minutes passed and I couldn't handle remaining idle.

"So, should we go see if your house was burned down, too?" I asked, which was clearly the wrong thing to say given the glare I received as reply.

Finn didn't reply. He pressed his palms against the rock once more before slamming his fist into it. As the boulder shattered, I was flung backward into the soot, landing on my ass with elbows down so my head didn't hit the ground.

"What the—" I started to say until my fingers got tangled in hair. Holy shit, actual hair.

I scrambled up and backed into Finn as he growled. "What?"

Words were lost on me as I recognized the longer strands of brunette hair wrapped around remnants of twigs from the trees no longer standing. I pointed to where I'd just been, unable to see anything other than the tip of a scorched nose and hair.

Finn roared, a blast of agony escaping him unlike anything I'd ever felt. Maddox was his family, and he was dead. I'd never grieved anyone other than the home I once thought I wanted. I was frozen in position as Finn's emotions choked me and I tried to figure out what to do with them.

He was digging into the ground, trying to get to Maddox, and glanced back at me with a fury in his eyes. "Care to help?"

I wasn't sure if the anger was directed toward me or at the situation. Either way, it broke the stupor I was in, and I got back on the ground.

Minutes later, we had the top half of Maddox exposed, but he wasn't moving. I reached a hand to Finn, but he flinched away. "He's not dead," he muttered before continuing to dig.

When we got to Maddox's waist, I wrapped my arms under his and held my breath as I pulled up on the body. He was still lifeless.

"Finn, I'm sorry," I said softly, truly meaning it for maybe the first time in my life.

"Are you, though? You thought of him as a traitor. You didn't even like him." His words were harsh and not untrue. It wasn't that I'd hated the fae. Hell, he'd helped me on several occasions, but I did doubt his loyalties more than once.

Given we were supposed to be mates, Finn's aggression toward me actually stung, but I didn't dwell on it. His friend was dead, and pain made people do stupid shit sometimes. Like be an asshole. I would know.

Finn gave Maddox his attention again, and I did the same, surprised to find there were no burn marks on him anywhere other than his face. His wings were out and damaged, but still attached. Seeing that Finn was cleaning Maddox up, I tried to help by bending down to straighten one of the gossamer extensions.

Next, I used both hands to brush the knotted hair away from his face, my fingers brushing over his skin, taking extra care to be gentle and not upset Finn even further. Then, a jolt rolled through me that was beyond my control, and Maddox's body jerked.

"What did you do to him?" Finn roared in my face.

I held my hands up, backing away. "I was just trying to help."

"Well, stop." His eyes were charcoal, and there was so much hatred there that I didn't even recognize the fae I thought Finn was. Hurt welled inside me at his rejection, and I moved even further from them until I heard a groan that didn't belong to either of us.

I stared down at Maddox's body, the one I had been certain was a corpse just seconds before, only to find his arms and wings beginning to move.

Finn lifted him up, patting Maddox's back and trying to coax words from his almost brother-in-law.

"Come on. Ivy needs you to be okay. You have to be okay, Maddox."

I no longer felt welcome, so I made myself scarce, choosing to watch from a distance. Maddox opened his eyes, a passion within them I recognized as something I held within me. They spoke in quiet voices, Maddox occasionally turning to glance at me, but still, nobody called me closer.

When I realized Maddox was okay enough, I began to focus on me. Sometime in the last twenty-four hours, I'd let a few of the bricks go from my wall that kept people away. Just a few layers, but it was a few too many. Even with my doubts, Finn's ire toward me wasn't something I wanted to let any further in.

Brick by brick, I put those layers back. I couldn't jump right into this bond. I couldn't let Finn have a hold on my emotions and actions. I needed my space like he needed his, and this was the only way I knew how to get it without feeling as if I was ripping my heart out.

Finn might have thought he could accept me, but he'd been lying to himself. We were two different fae and, regardless of what fate had in store for us, being bonded didn't seem to be in anyone's best interest.

CHAPTER 7

Maddox couldn't walk on his own, but he was at least breathing, which was a hell of a lot more than I expected when we first found him. His throat had been crushed under the dirt and rock, so he could barely speak above a whisper, but none of that mattered much. I was still keeping my distance.

Finn hadn't even glanced my way before announcing we were headed for his place. With my wall in place and my give-a-damn buried where it belonged, I grabbed on to Finn's arm. I had forgotten to ask where the safe places were that we could teleport to.

When we arrived, we ended up in the bunker where Dave had made himself explode. Oh, how much I missed my relationship with Finn then. It was without real feelings and so much damn easier.

"I'm going to go take a look around outside. The two of you stay here," Finn stated after he settled

Maddox onto a blanket on the floor. There were no couches, so that was the next best place for him.

"Like hell I'm staying behind. If there are guards waiting for us to return, you're going to need my help." Finn had another thing coming if he thought he could boss me around.

"Lucinda, I don't need this right now. I just want to grab the encrypted tablet I use for email communication, and then we will go. I don't need you out there attracting attention."

"Is that all you think I'm good at? Creating chaos and making things worse?" My eyes glared at him, fury exploding within me, matching what I was sensing from him, regardless of the mental wall I'd created.

"Lucinda, please." His voice cracked, and I tossed my hands into the air.

"Whatever. Go do what you want while I'm here playing babysitter."

He didn't reply, and I didn't look his way again, but I heard every stomp he took up the stairs, counting each step until there were no more. Finn and I were already acting like the bitter married humans I'd seen on Earth, and we'd only been bonded for a day. This was just great.

I took a seat next to Maddox on the ground and gave him another once-over. His hair was matted, likely needing to be cut off. The burns were limited to his face, bubbled, charred, and hideous. "I'm sorry I thought you were a traitor, but I'm glad you're not dead," I said when he caught me staring.

Maddox choked, trying not to laugh. "Thanks, I

think. I just need to see a healer so we can get Ivy back." His voice was still hoarse and low, but the words at least made sense.

"So not to be rude, but how are you not dead? You were buried for two days, unless you'd done that to yourself later on." If I couldn't be outside, a little conversation was going to be necessary.

He tried to turn toward me but winced in pain before staying put. "Well, I think I was. Or, at least in some sort of stasis. I don't know. I walked in a world with no feeling, no color, no sound, no nothing. I walked for what seemed like days, trying to find a way out. Then, my body felt like it was hit with electricity and the pain returned."

I opened my mouth to ask more questions, but I heard a shout from above. I tensed, glancing at Maddox. "Go," was all he said.

Even though Finn was being a dick, I wasn't going to leave him out there alone. I charged for the stairs, unfurling my wings and keeping them close at my sides. The door was cracked from Finn's earlier departure, and a sliver of light shone through. Using more force than intended, I pushed through and ignored the crack of the door hitting the building.

There were five guards fighting Finn all at the same time right outside the house. The rest of the farm was still smoldering from a recent fire, but I couldn't focus on what was around me. My heart constricted as I watched two of the guards hold on to Finn's wings and a third blast his chest with magic.

My mate was bleeding and hurting. The bond took

over as a wave of crimson settled over my vision and I couldn't think about anything other than killing those who thought they could hurt what was mine.

A guttural roar ripped from my throat as I sprinted forward, acting like an animalistic shifter with no humanity. The bond instincts were so much more than I could have predicted. Power poured from me in waves as shocks of magic arced around my fingertips and I lost control of my actions. Two of the five came for me, but that wasn't enough. There would never be enough of them to stop me from saving Finn.

I was no longer just a fae. Within an instant, I'd become a ferocious beast who only cared about keeping her treasure safe. It didn't matter that Finn had just treated me like shit. It didn't matter that I wasn't loving the bond. All that I could focus on was making sure he stayed alive.

I wrapped my fingers around the throat of the first fae attempting to attack me and used my hardened wings to block a blast from the second. Without hesitating, I ripped the head off the first and sliced a gaping hole into the chest of the other.

My wings were expanded as far as they could reach as I crept toward the remaining three, still holding Finn.

"Come any closer and I'll take his head off," the one who was standing in front snarled.

I laughed in return, the sound unlike anything I'd ever made before. "I don't think so."

I plucked one of my feathers and sent it sailing toward the unknown fae, watching as it sank into his neck and blood began to gush out. The cowardice fae disappeared, but I didn't care. He'd never make it to a healer in time, and he wouldn't be able to speak with the feather lodged in the middle of his throat, so he was no longer a threat.

The two crouched behind Finn as I met his gaze. There was a hunger in his eyes I'd never seen before, but also a rage I could relate to. He shook his head, but I didn't know what he was trying to tell me. If he thought I wasn't going to kill these assholes, he was sorely mistaken.

As I used my wings to propel me forward, Finn jerked out of their hold and snapped the neck of one just as I landed on the other. Finn was too close, and my wings cut into his arm when I lifted them to behead the last remaining guard.

Finn hissed in pain and grunted before shoving the fae he'd killed to the ground and heading inside. Before he disappeared completely, I caught him glance back at me, but neither of us said anything, his face unreadable.

Whatever. He could be pissed off all he wanted, but I'd been right. He had needed me, and he shouldn't have shut me out. After double-checking that there were no other fae around, I started to take deep breaths, slowing my heart rate and trying to calm the adrenaline pumping through my veins.

My focus stayed on the smoke coming from the orchards around the house. It appeared as if we'd shown up just in time to prevent them from burning down Finn's house next. It was the only thing left untouched that I could see.

As Finn's safety registered with me, the

overwhelming sense of protectiveness began wearing off. I wanted to throat punch myself for how I'd acted. I hated that the bond had so much control over my actions. I was supposed to be pissed at Finn for being an asshole, but instead, I wanted nothing more than to wrap my arms around him. It was an awful feeling. What was even worse was realizing that no matter how much I hated how I felt, I also understood the truth of our situation.

I needed him even if I wanted to hate him.

That didn't mean I would forget how he treated me, though. It just meant I wasn't going to run away because things were hard. No, he was going to hear what I thought about his shit attitude and that he needed to do something about it. If he continued to be difficult, then I was going to show him how versed I was at being a pain in the ass.

Finn was back within seconds, tablet in his grasp. He took my hand and pulled me along, still not speaking to me. While I really wanted to say something right then, I knew we had to get Maddox back to the island where he could heal.

Maddox's mouth downturned when he saw us. "If you haven't already, the two of you better make it to the bedroom soon. The tension is suffocating."

Finn snarled. "Shut your mouth before I leave you here."

I leaned down, helping him up. "Don't worry, Maddie. I wouldn't leave you behind." I waved at Finn and disappeared with Maddox in tow. Just because I was willing to keep quiet about my irritation didn't mean I wouldn't show it.

Finn was only half a second behind us and practically dripping in rage when we appeared on the island. We arrived in front of Mosi and Olida's hut, both of them coming out as Finn stared me down.

"Oh, dear. Bring him inside," Olida fussed, and Finn took Maddox from me with more force than necessary. I stayed outside, not wanting to crowd Olida while she worked and also needing some space from Finn.

Mosi watched me with curiosity and a grin on his face. I waltzed toward him and poked a finger at his chest as I remembered what Finn had told me before we left. "I don't like people using magic on me without my permission. I don't care if you're like me or not."

He nodded, seeming to understand what I meant. "The mark cannot do you any harm. Don't worry about that. Did you learn anything while you were gone?"

My brows pinched in confusion. "Uh, no. Were we supposed to?"

Mosi kicked a twig, avoiding my stare. "Possibly. We'll see." He turned around and went back inside his home.

My chest rumbled. I was beyond done with the day, and it was still morning.

I HADN'T STUCK AROUND LONG. INSTEAD, I VENTURED through the trees, meeting a few of the island fae. They were all nice enough but had no idea what was happening in the real world. The fact that the fae here were okay with that didn't sit well with me. How could someone not care that the person who promised to take care of their kind was killing them instead? I just couldn't understand.

Then again, most people didn't understand me, either. I tried not to let it get me even more riled up.

When I was done, I found myself at the beach again, sitting on the same log and watching the waves. I'd been there about an hour when a soft humming noise caught my attention.

I turned around to find Olida walking toward me. She was freshly bathed from the soap smell I caught and had a smile on her face.

"I take it Maddox is okay?" I asked, trying not to be disappointed that Finn hadn't come to find me first.

"He is. While he won't be leaving bed today, he will make a full recovery with minimal scars and less hair."

The burns on his face flashed through my mind and I cringed.

"How are you doing?" she asked after taking a seat next to me, digging her bare feet into the sand.

"Why did you follow me out here again?" I didn't want to lie or tell her the truth, so I answered the question with one of my own instead.

She hesitated before responding, making me wonder if she was trying to come up with a lie. "I don't know," she finally said.

Well, that didn't make me feel great.

She continued, "I'm drawn to you. Your power is unlike any I've encountered before. It's similar to my

Mosi's, but I think that's because you're both feathered fae—special."

I scoffed. "I'm not special. I can't do anything that nobody else can."

"At least, not that you know of. You're still young and finding your place in this world, Lucy. Give it time, and when you least expect it, a gift will appear. Like Finn did."

My stomach twisted with something I didn't recognize. "I'm not so sure Finn is a gift. I think we were put together to torture each other for all eternity."

Olida laughed so hard, she had to hold her stomach. When I glared at her, she sobered, but only a little. "I'm sorry, dear. I don't mean to make light of the situation, but the two of you remind me so much of me and Mosi. That first year… Oh, lordy. I wanted to murder him, and I'd never even considered hurting a fly before. Being bonded is not easy. Especially with a past like yours. You will have your trials and tribulations, but if you can stick with it, the rewards will be more than you ever imagined."

I wanted to believe her, but we were not the same.

"I promise I didn't come here to preach or make you feel better. You're allowed to wallow in your own feelings if you choose to. I just wanted to let you know that we were done and Finn was showering. Also, I believe there were messages from your elf friend that he found."

With everything else happening, I'd almost forgotten about the emails we needed to read. "Is she okay? Did she find a witch?"

"Finn didn't really read them. It seemed as if he wanted to wait for you. I'd hurry back and see what's what. Before you decide to hold on to this anger, remember he's been through a lot the last few days, too. That mate of yours has watched his sister be kidnapped, thought you were going to die, and now seen his best friend on death's door as well. He might need you more than he's willing to say. The two of you really aren't that different."

Ha! The thought of Finn needing me for anything other than assisting in a fight wasn't something I could envision.

I did want to read the emails from Neva and set a time to get her, so I stood up, ready to do just that. She'd been gone too long. It was time to get my elf back.

CHAPTER 8

*W*hen we arrived back at the main part of the island, fae were roaming freely. Each of them smiled and nodded, saying hello in their own ways. I'd never been welcomed in this way. I'd always been shamed for being different, but there wasn't an ounce of that here. I tried to ignore the warmth that bloomed in my chest as I was around these people longer, but it was getting harder.

Once I entered Olida and Mosi's hut, I found Maddox resting on a single bed that was taking up the area where we'd sat during my first visit into their home. Finn was there, too, standing by Maddox's side, holding the tablet. His stare was on me instead of the screen.

When our eyes met, my chest constricted and my throat tightened with emotions, not all of which I knew how to identify. All of these "things" that came with the bond were not what I was expecting. I missed the days when I didn't care about anything. I actually missed the voice inside my head who often agreed with me. Or maybe it had been me agreeing with it. Either way, I'd always known what to expect before.

Anxiety crept its way through my body until my hands shook and I found it hard to breathe. Finn was watching me, a pained expression on his face. "Luc—"

I didn't hear the rest. I needed another minute to myself before I let the bond get the better of me. I had to get my shit under control before I did something that would make me hate myself.

I darted out the door, going around to the back of the hut, hoping to be left alone. Kneeling over, I put my head low and took deep breaths. Gods, this was the fucking worst. Why in the world did people continuously look for love? There was literally nothing appealing about caring for others so much it made you sick.

A warm hand rubbed my back and my heart beat faster, sensing it was Finn before I even looked up.

"I'm sorry, Lucinda," he whispered, bending closer to me.

I jerked up and shoved him away, ignoring how his closeness made me feel. "I don't think so, asshole. Do you even know what you're sorry for?"

"For dismissing your help when I should have trusted your instincts," he said confidently.

My head shook, and I kept my voice lethal and low to avoid being overheard. Our business wasn't for anyone else's entertainment. "How about when you accused me of further hurting Maddox? Or the way your eyes cast down at me afterward, still seeing me like the monster I know you believed me to be? Or maybe for when you ignored me several times over?"

He at least winced at my words. Good. I hoped he felt like shit, because that was how he'd made me feel.

"Lucy, listen," he begged.

I waved my hand in the air. "No, I don't want to listen. I didn't want any of this. You showed up, asking for my help. I only agreed because it meant I could kill the king. Never once did I ask for anything more. And now… I'm suddenly bonded and caring for others, but why? Why would I willingly subject myself to this hurt, Finn? I'm so done with it."

He moved quickly, grabbing on to my arms and pressing his body against me. "I'm sorry. For all of it. More than you know. Please, don't leave."

I sneered at him. "I don't believe you."

Finn took my hand and pressed it against his chest; his heart was pounding beneath my touch. "Only you have ever made me second-guess myself. Only you have made my heart do this. Only you have made me want to change the world. I need you to believe me, Lucy."

Tension slowly left my body as his liquid eyes bored into my soul and the heat of his body began to thaw mine. The longer he held me, the stronger the bond grew, but I fought it off. I wanted to be pissed. Hell, I deserved to be.

"You can't treat me the way you did today and expect me to stick around. I don't know how to do any of this. I will always believe I'm better off alone if I have no proof otherwise. I *need* you to convince me it's better to stay if that's what you really want, but not just because of the bond. It's not like it has to be forever. You're not stuck with me if that's what you believe," I said.

His forehead pressed against mine, and he took a deep breath. "I was furious today, but not for the reasons you think. I truly am sorry for allowing you to believe them. You are everything I am not, and there is nothing wrong with that. In fact, it has only made me want you more since the moment I saw you in LA."

His fingers brushed away my hair that had fallen into my eyes, and I sucked in a breath at the power igniting between us. Made even stronger with the tension brought on by the day's events.

He continued, "I'd actually agreed with you at one point. I'd believed Maddox had left us the day Edgar had shown up. I'd lost my faith in him. Then, I'd lost it in myself and my ability to keep Ivy safe once she was gone. After I spoke with Mosi and knew the truth, I ignored how it made me feel for as long as I could. But finding Maddox's body, I couldn't hold it all in any longer."

I gripped his shirt, feeling sorry for him, and then immediately being angry at myself for beginning to forgive him. I wanted to be furious enough with him to walk away, but that option was becoming harder as the hours ticked by. His eyes briefly closed, and the twinge in his cheek was back, something I thought I'd missed but hated seeing now.

Finn gently pressed his lips to my forehead. "I took my anger toward myself out on you, and that wasn't fair. You're not the only one struggling with this bond. Don't get me wrong. I promise that I've come to accept you for who you are, and I absolutely do not want to break it—that isn't something I would ever lie to you about. Of course, I hope there will be a little less killing in your future, but if it needs to be done to keep others safe, I understand that is part of who you are. My problem mostly lies with not being sure I'm good enough for you as a mate, and that guts me."

My fingers grasped his chin. "Finn, you are one of the kindest fae I know, with a moral compass unlike any I've ever met. Why in the world would you think you're not good enough for me?"

"My kindness has done nothing but nearly get people killed," he spat.

I lifted up onto my toes, trying to get eye level with him. "Your kindness is going to change the world." Then, I pressed my lips to his, and that was all he needed to take control. His fingers sank into my hair, angling my head as he deepened the kiss.

My hands ventured around to his back, my nails digging into his skin as I held on tight.

He slowed down, once again resting his head on mine. "I came out here to make you feel better and you ended up comforting me. I'm sorry. Again."

I patted his chest. "You don't need to keep apologizing. I believe you feel bad, but don't mistake that kiss as me forgetting what happened today. I understand your reasons now, but it doesn't mean your earlier actions hurt me any less. We're not always going to agree. We are as opposite as two fae can get. Yet, as it's been pointed out, we are also very alike. I'm still not sold on this bond idea and how it controls me, but I learned enough today to know I want to see what happens by sticking around for a while longer."

He squeezed me tighter, nuzzling my neck. "The way you rarely hold things back is admirable, and I promise not to shut you out anymore."

I was on emotional overload and needed space, so I calmly pushed him back. "Can we please be done with the heavy today and go get my elf?"

Finn dropped his arms, respecting my wants. "I would love nothing more."

I followed him back inside the hut where Maddox was sitting up in bed. "You two done acting like children?"

"You done being ugly yet?" I asked in return, feeling more like myself.

He shrugged. "The hair will grow back, and I've been told chicks dig scars. Hopefully, Ivy won't mind looking at mine for the rest of our lives."

That was not where I wanted the conversation to head. As much as I hoped Ivy was okay, I couldn't take any more emotional conversations. I felt for Maddox, and I would find a way to free Ivy from Zephyr if it was possible. Unfortunately, that time hadn't come yet, and I couldn't guarantee she'd survive.

"So, how about those emails?" I asked, searching for the tablet.

Olida handed it to me. "I was going to try and read them, not knowing how long you two would be gone, but your fancy technology is not something I will ever understand."

Finn leaned over and typed in the code to unlock the screen while I smiled at Olida. I really did enjoy her company. She reminded me of the kind of mother I always wished for as a child.

Once the screen was unlocked, the email inbox was the first thing I saw. There were six short messages from the elf. They began polite and moved on to more frustrated emotions when we weren't responding.

First one came the second evening she was gone: *I finally got in touch with Beatrix. She said she would help, but there are conditions I'm not sure Ms. Lucinda will like. I'll send the full list as soon as I have them.*

Two hours after the first: *Never mind. Beatrix is having more problems with the vampires. She's out. But she gave a few names and I'm going to look into them tomorrow.*

The following afternoon: *First two witches nearly killed me. Why isn't anyone responding to these messages?*

Several hours later: *Lucinda Morrow, I'm going to give away Black Widow.*

The next morning: *If you've gone after the king on your own, we're going to have words, Ms. Lucinda. I didn't sign up for this. I'm about ready for my sock.*

That one made me snort out loud. "You just had to give her the ammunition for that one, didn't you?" I asked Finn, and he grinned as we kept reading.

Last message was sent just twelve hours prior: *I found an ally. Not sure what to do now. He's a little skittish, so a reply soon would be helpful. We're running out of options. If you're not dead, you better have a good reason for ignoring me. I'll find a way back to the fae realm if I don't hear from you within the next day. I need to know what's going on.*

I hit the reply button: *We're alive.* Then, send.

"That's all you're going to tell her?" Finn asked.

"No, but at least she will have that while I type a longer response. We don't need her trying to barge into the realm and getting herself killed." Then, I formed a new email, summarizing the chaos and telling her we would meet in Sri Lanka that evening. Dusk was only a couple hours away, and having the cover of night was preferable.

By the time I tapped "send" a second time, there was a response from Neva: *You've got to be kidding me. I've been working day and night to help all of you and after days of wondering if you're dead, your only response is "We're alive". I quit. That's it. I'm done. Good luck to you all.*

My brow raised. "I guess I found where her patience ends."

Finn seemed more concerned than me. "Do you think she'll even read the more proper email?"

Maddox was trying to lean out of the bed. "What's happening? What did you guys do?"

I waved him off. "Oh hush, fairy. Everything is fine. Neva is just a little upset. She'll be fine."

Minutes passed, and the silence became thick as we waited for another reply. Shit, maybe I really had pushed Neva beyond her breaking point.

"Should I go back to LA?" I asked.

Mosi shook his head. He'd been quiet in the corner,

sketching in a notepad throughout all of it. "You can't go back there until… well, just not yet," he said without looking up.

Well, that answered that. Not.

I'd trust Mosi's opinion for the time being, but only because I adored his mate.

The tablet dinged with a new message. Finn read it first and sighed, then handed it over.

I'm glad you're not dead. I withdraw my resignation and we will see you tonight.

Her message was short, and I knew I was still going to get a talking to once she was back, but I didn't even care. I hadn't realized how much I would miss her being around when I'd sent her away. Having her back would be a good thing for everyone.

Finn relayed the information to Maddox while I grabbed a cup of tea. Except, when I took a sip, my eyes met Olida's and I knew it wasn't just tea.

She held a finger to her lips and winked.

"You're wicked and I like it," I whispered.

"I'm not wicked, but I do like my fun. Adding a bit of spice to the island life is necessary for my sanity. Without these," she held her cup up, "I'd never survive."

"When all this is over, I'm going to convince you to leave this island," I replied.

"And I just might let you."

e spent the next few hours sitting with Maddox while Olida and Mosi came and went. They still had things to take care of, and it was nice to have them focusing on something other than us.

"So, we'll teleport to the island and then have to fly back. As long as Neva is already there with the witch, then we should be back within a couple of hours," Finn said to Maddox.

Gods, sometimes magic was helpful and sometimes it was annoying. I hated that the fae realm was the only place we couldn't teleport into. At least, not that I knew of. But at the same time, it kept our world safer. As soon as King Douche was removed from being in charge, that would be a bigger deal to the rest of its residents.

"I'm fine. I can come with you guys," Maddox said, sitting up and trying to swing his legs off the bed.

"Maddox Adams, you move one step out of that bed, and it will be the last you take," Olida threatened, making him pause as she entered the hut.

Maddox slowly swiveled his head to meet her stare and cringed before throwing himself back and sighing loudly. He was pretty high on whatever juju Olida had used on him, and it was keeping him in a decent mood, but I knew that would be short-lived once he was healed up. He'd already had small bouts of rage throughout the day about us not going to Ivy first.

"Well, that's our cue to leave," I said, tugging on Finn. "Let's go."

"Don't worry, I'll keep an eye on this one." Olida waved as we shut the door behind us.

Finn stepped next to me. "We'll need to go outside of the protective shield and then to the realm barrier. Do you want to take the lead and I'll watch behind us? I'm sure us killing those guards at my house didn't go unnoticed."

"You lead and I'll watch. I'm faster than you if someone does see us."

He opened his mouth to likely argue and then sighed. "Just don't take off without me if you see anything."

I patted his chest. "I'll do my best."

"Why doesn't that make me feel any better?" Finn groaned.

"Because it wasn't supposed to." I winked and unfurled my wings, pushing into the sky with Finn right behind me.

The setting sun cast purple rays into the sky that reflected off Finn's forest-green wings, showcasing the scars he'd received since meeting me. When I'd first seen them, they'd been free of blemishes, and I felt a twinge of guilt that I was partly responsible for the new appearances.

Though, I didn't focus on them for long. I knew there was a hunt going on for us. We had to be focused and ready for anything. I called my power forth until teal streams circled around my hands and my arms.

"Mosi asked that we teleport around a little bit to throw the guards off with their searches. The island here can't be found, but the movements should keep some of the other fae on the islands safer from Zephyr's wrath," Finn said, reaching for my hand.

"Lead the way, then." Teleporting didn't take much energy, and it could be fun if we ran into any guards.

We first appeared much too close to the castle. I began to speak, ready to chastise Finn for bringing us there, but the air was pulled from my lungs as we disappeared again. Next, we were by South Island, and I wondered about the decimated lands there. Was everything dead now? Had the fae been smart enough to leave yet? That wasn't a concern I had the time to confirm just then.

We were back at West Island, but this time right on the beach nearest to the castle. "What the fu—"

"I'm sorry, what was that?" Finn asked as we appeared on North Island.

"You're going to pay for this." I tried to rip my hand from his so he couldn't take me with him, but his grip tightened, and we disappeared once more.

"Last stop before exiting," he said, glancing around. "Shit. Just kidding."

I turned in time to see guards coming toward us but

couldn't do anything before we teleported again. Finn did this three more times before we ended up on a remote island.

"Fly. Fast." He pushed into the air and I followed, keeping pace with him and heading straight for the barrier. We just had to get through and hope nobody followed.

A blast of magic hit my boot, and I hissed. A split second after I slowed to turn around, Finn latched on to me. "No, you don't. We're almost there and they won't follow."

"How do you know that?"

Finn didn't answer. Instead, he shoved me through the barrier, and then we teleported one last time. We were both out of breath but standing on a dock at the tip of the island that was Sri Lanka and, according to him, safe.

I went to ask my question again, but he held up his finger, moving us out of view behind a shed. Just when I was ready to throat punch him, a group of humans walked by and I hid my wings. They were drunk and not paying attention, so it didn't much matter, but we were better safe than sorry.

"Rumors. That's how I know the guards won't follow us. King Zephyr never sent anyone after you, because word got around that you'd made friends with the shifters and witches. He's never had enough men to fight you *and* them while expecting to win."

Ahh, that made sense. I'd always wondered why I'd been left alone. Zephyr had known what I was capable of, that I was a liability. But I'd never worried enough to dig into it as long as I was able to live my life as I saw fit on Earth.

"Okay, then. Now, where is Neva and this witch?" I asked as we stepped out of the shadows and into the moonlight filtering down from the dark sky.

Power rushed over me, a kind I didn't recognize and much too strong for it to be anything good. In an instant, my wings were back out. My muscles ached from the pressure of whatever was pushing down on us. "Did you feel that?" I murmured, and he nodded.

We kept watch while I tried to sense where the surge had come from, but it was as if it didn't exist any longer. I took a step forward and slammed into something hard. "What the hell?"

"Not witch," a man's voice demanded, deep and with a slight Russian accent.

"What?" I asked, frustrated I couldn't see the man the voice belonged to.

"You call me a witch. I am not," he grumbled.

"Good to know. Neva?" I called.

"Right here." I heard her voice but couldn't see her.

My hands ventured to the left, toward the sound, and I felt her soft curls, then grabbed her shoulder and pulled her closer. "Why can't I see you, little elf?" My voice laced with anger toward the "not witch" she'd arrived with.

"Yury doesn't like people he's never met before," she replied.

I scoffed in feigned surprise. "You don't say? Well, Yury who is not a witch, it would be great if you could show yourself and my friend. You know, so we can get going."

Magic, just as strong as before, swirled around us in a fog. I still held on to Neva, and Finn was at my side, letting me take the lead. Once the smoke cleared, Neva's round umber face came into view. She appeared unharmed.

I cast my attention to Yury, wondering what the hell he was if not a witch, because he certainly put off witchy vibes.

He was nearly as tall as Finn, completely bald, and a centimeter away from having a thick unibrow with how tightly scrunched his face was. His midnight eyes met mine, appraising me just as I was him. His light skin was scarred, but nothing so damaging that someone would notice at first glance. Just faint white lines that caught my attention.

He wore all black, beginning with his long-sleeve t-shirt and all the way down to his sandals with socks. Interesting choice, which I wanted to point out, but since he was helping us, I figured it wasn't the time.

"Lucinda Morrow," he grunted.

"Yury, the not witch," I replied.

"I'm a sorcerer, and you will address me as such if you want my help." The beast of a man put his attention on Finn. "You are Finn Barlow?"

"I am."

"Good. Both of you, hold still." Yury rubbed his palms together, magic sparking between them, and then he stepped closer, placing one hand on my chest and the other on Finn's. At first, I thought maybe he was copping a feel, but then Neva backed up and my body began to shake.

"Stay still," Yury demanded as if I was meaning to convulse.

"Neva," I called through clenched teeth.

"I'm sorry, Ms. Lucinda. He said I couldn't warn you. If I did, he wouldn't help Ivy."

Nodding, I trusted her. She would have done her best to vet this sorcerer and, assuming Beatrix told her about him, I had to at least attempt to believe he wasn't trying to kill us.

Finn reached for my hand, but Yury's knee darted up, blocking the contact. "No touching."

Another half-minute later, he released us, and I backed up several paces. "Yury, not a witch who doesn't like people. While I can appreciate your help, you ever touch me without my permission again and I'll take your head off."

He nodded. "I respect that. Now we go."

Finn stepped forward. "Wait a minute. What did you just do to us?"

Solid question that I maybe should have led with.

"I masked your power. I don't want to be found, meaning you need to be hidden."

Neva nodded. "It's like the spell Beatrix gave to you, but longer lasting. He did the same to me."

She seemed to add the last part as validation for bringing this crazy-ass sorcerer into our lives, but I wasn't going to blame Neva for any actions he might take. I was happy to take those aggressions out on Beatrix if anything went wrong.

Yury's hands began to move once more, and a portal opened. I'd never actually seen one in person considering fae couldn't do them, and I was moderately impressed. It was probably ten feet tall and three feet wide with white fog forming around the perimeter. When I peeked closer, all I could see was ocean. "Where is this?"

"Near your realm entrance. Should be minutes from your home," Yury answered.

"Have you been to Fae Islands?" Finn asked.

"I don't need to have been there to sense its magical presence," he replied, indignation coating his words. "Are you capable of flying with me? I am powerful, but I cannot fly and do not like water."

I was pretty sure there was an underlying threat in there, but Finn didn't seem bothered. "Of course, I can." He turned to me. "You'll take Neva, and we can all stick together?"

I nodded. "Sure thing."

Yury grabbed on to Finn's arm as Neva stepped closer to me. "You seem different. So does Mr. Finn. Are you sure the two of you are okay?" she asked quietly.

I hadn't told her that I'd bonded with Finn in my email, and I certainly wasn't going to tell her around the not-witch we didn't know. That was something she could figure out later.

"Things might have changed, but we're okay." I stepped forward with Neva in my grasp and moved my wings as soon as we entered the portal. I only lost a few feet of air before we stabilized and then watched as Yury closed the opening with a snap of his fingers.

Finn led the way and, sure enough, we were back at the fae entrance within ten minutes, but Finn hesitated and glanced down at Yury. "Don't try to kill me when we teleport."

"Don't do anything stupid and I won't," the sorcerer deadpanned.

I followed immediately behind as Finn ignored the comment and we all went into the fae realm. Once we each appeared, I waited a moment before moving. We'd been chased before we left. This would be a true test of Yury's power if none of the guards appeared.

"What are we waiting for?" Yury complained, dangling from Finn's hands.

"To see how well your spell works. We can't lead the bad guys to the good guys. That would be rude," I replied.

"My power is infallible. Keep moving. Your waiting is the only reason we will be found," he grunted.

Finn seemed to think that was good enough, teleporting first, and I followed behind. As we crossed through the protective barrier, we flew toward the beach instead of the main part of the island.

"Where are we?" Neva asked, and I grinned.

"Somewhere you will be safe while we kill the bad guys."

She shook her head. "Okay, maybe you haven't changed all that much."

As soon as we landed, Yury moved swiftly away from Finn, dusting himself off like he'd been contaminated. "I will be in the trees. Do not call for me until you have the girl." The sorcerer snapped his fingers and disappeared.

"Well, isn't he a peach. Makes me look like a saint," I added with a laugh.

"I wouldn't go that far, but I do appreciate your company more after spending an extended amount of time in his," Neva replied as we walked next to Finn.

"Let's go tell the others we're back early." Finn reached for my hand, and Neva raised a brow at me, not having missed the action.

"Later," I mouthed and kept walking.

Something told me that particular conversation with Neva wasn't going to be my favorite, and I had no problem avoiding it for as long as I could.

ith Yury hiding like some psycho in the jungle, we went straight to Mosi and Olida. Neva was acting like a kid at a theme park for the first time as we walked to the hut, letting her take it all in.

"I've never seen flowers this vibrant. Oh, is that a monkey? What kind of bird is that?" she asked, having all of the questions that we didn't really have the answers for. I had a feeling she and Olida would be spending a lot of time together. Hopefully, some of Olida's mischievousness would rub off on my much-too-polite brownie elf.

A question of my own arose. "How did Yury get through the barrier Mosi created?"

"Mosi gave me the... uh, magical permission to let people in. Neva shouldn't have been able to get in, either, but a simple touch of power and apparently all is well. Didn't make this place sound very safe, but Mosi assured me it still was."

Well, at least Finn wasn't completely drunk on the Mosi juice like the fae who lived here. Not that I disagreed with their loyalty, but people really should ask more questions before entrusting their lives to someone.

We kept walking, and Neva changed the subject from her curiosity about all things "secret island" to me. "You know, I haven't forgotten how mad I was at you."

"Does it help if I say I'm sorry?" I replied, realizing I'd been throwing that word around a lot lately. That was something I would have to ponder on my own soon.

She stopped walking, mouth hanging open.

Finn and I paused, turning to face her. "What?" I asked.

She still gaped. "I think you actually meant that."

My arms shrugged, remaining casual in hopes she didn't make a huge deal out of nothing. "Probably." I truly hadn't enjoyed worrying her. Sure, riling her up with things that pushed her prim and proper boundaries were enjoyable, but having her believe we were dead wasn't a line I had purposely crossed.

Neva stepped closer, finger raised at me. "What happened to you?"

Finn tugged on my elbow. "I hear Mosi. We should hurry up. He'll need to know there's a sorcerer on his island before one or more of his men accidentally get themselves killed."

Saved by the mate.

Neva was even more suspicious but kept walking with us. I'd sit to talk with her at some point, but I wanted to know what came next before that happened. Mosi hadn't been very forthcoming with his visions previously and, if he didn't have anything more for us now, I was going to insist we leave.

Not that I didn't necessarily trust Mosi, but the longer we stayed away from the castle, the more Ivy's image appeared in my mind. Seeing her within the king's grasp, her determined eyes that told me she was okay with dying, and worst of all, the way he'd threatened to torture her in front of me.

I might not have qualms about her dying if Yury couldn't do his job, but allowing Ivy to suffer when we were capable of storming the castle once again was eating away at me more and more as time passed.

When we approached the main circle of huts, Mosi was indeed outside and waiting for us. "It's time for you to leave," he said, shocking the shit out of me.

"Well, that's rude," I replied.

Mosi fought a smile. "But come inside first."

"Do you think it's Yury? Should I have not brought him here?" Neva whispered, her honey eyes wide.

"If it has anything to do with one of us, I'm sure it's me. Don't worry," I replied as Finn coughed to cover up a laugh next to me.

Neva's unease didn't lessen as we entered the hut. Olida was already there, food in a hand and a smile in place.

"Oh, dear! You must be Neva." Olida glanced at me and winked. "You didn't deserve her. I can sense how pure she is from here."

"I won't argue with you on that," I replied as Neva tried to take in all that was happening around her.

Maddox was no longer inside the hut, and neither was the bed they'd brought in for him. The floor pillows that served as the faes' only offered seating were back, and I took a seat, hoping to get our conversation going quickly. Finn followed my lead, and Neva finally joined us once Mosi and Olida sat as well.

"There is a sorcerer hiding in your jungle. He's friendly. I think," Finn said first.

Mosi nodded. "Yury will not be a problem."

"How did you..." Neva began, but I interrupted.

"Mosi can see possible futures. He doesn't actually say everything he knows, but he usually knows, and it can be annoying."

"I see," she replied.

"No, he does." I snorted at my own joke, but nobody else did. Party downers. "So, why do we need to leave?"

Olida handed out mugs, and I was disappointed to find it wasn't her special tea or more hot toddies.

"You have everything you need now. Maddox is healed and bathing in our purified waters. Neva is here. There is a sorcerer standing by to hopefully help Ivy, and the two of you are bonded. There are no—"

Mosi was cut off by Neva spitting her tea all over his lap. "What did you just say?" Then, her hands covered her mouth as she realized what she'd done. "I'm so sorry," she mumbled.

"Did I leave that part out? My bad," I said while Olida got a towel for her mate.

Neva punched me in the arm, and it actually hurt. "Damn, elf. For a tiny thing, you know how to throw a punch."

"You're on my shit list," she snapped.

I feigned shock. "Language, Neva."

"No. I can't with you right now." She turned to Mosi. "I really am very sorry, Mr. Mosi. Ms. Lucinda failed to tell me of her bonding to Mr. Finn. I did not mean to disrespect you."

He laughed as he wiped his lap. "Oh, Neva. I've seen you, and you're going to be alright. I promise."

A part of me breathed a sigh of relief as Neva seemed to get slightly more nervous. Was Mosi giving insight to the future? If Neva stayed with us, would she be safe from the crossfire? I didn't know for sure, but I would roll with it for the time being.

"And no more formalities. Just Mosi is fine," he added once he was cleaned up.

I didn't even bother telling him to save his breath. Neva was proper, through and through.

Olida nudged him. "Get back on track, dear. They need to rest and prepare to leave while I plan our feast."

"Ah, yes. Let's continue."

Neva glared at me. Finn grinned. Olida's eyes twinkled. Everyone was having a blast, and we'd barely gotten started. Super.

"As I was saying, you've done everything needed so far to put you on the path that will lead to the best chance at beating Zephyr as of now. You will have one night's rest, and then there won't be much sleep in your future, so don't skip the opportunity. The islands are safe for you, but you can't come back here until you've entered the castle once again."

"You're kicking us out?" Finn asked.

"I'm guiding you," Mosi corrected. "I know it's hard to understand, but I've done everything I can up until this point. If I am needed, I will be there, but that is a path that has not been set yet. You first need to find the Renegades, at least what is left of them. Then, you'll know what to do from there."

"So, we're not saving my sister?" Finn's voice was rough, tension rolling off him in waves.

"You need to find the Renegades next. That is all I can say." Mosi at least appeared guilty for not giving us more information as his eyes pinched together and hands rubbed along his cotton pants.

"Well, that's bullshit," Neva stated, completely out of nowhere.

Olida burst into laughter. "Lucy, I think you brought back the wrong elf. She is nothing as you've described, and I love it!"

I reached a hand to Neva, and she pushed me away, tossing her curls out of her face and squaring her shoulders at me. "I've spent three days thinking every one of you were dead. Thinking everyone I'd met at Finn's was dead. That was not okay. I spent hours scouring the supernatural community trying to find someone to save Ivy, and now we don't even know if we're going to do that? I am not okay with any of this."

Mosi reached out, placing a hand on her knee. Power emanated from him, and she visibly calmed in her seat. "I'm sorry, Neva. You've worked very hard and you've done everything right. Your actions are not wasted and I'm sorry that you were worried."

Even Olida was somber as we waited for Neva's next reply. "I will accept that for now, but I'm not sorry for my outburst," she stated with confidence.

"And you shouldn't have to be," I replied. "So, we wait for Maddox to finish and leave?"

Olida tsked. "We shall hold a feast tonight, and you will rest here before your journey continues."

"You're throwing us a party," I said, then Mosi and Finn both groaned.

Olida held a hand to her chest. "I wouldn't dream of that. A party wouldn't be appropriate in these times, but we will indulge in the finer things the island has to offer." Then, she winked at me.

We were absolutely having a party.

Mosi stood first, and the rest of us followed. Olida went off to begin preparations, insisting she didn't need help from any of us, and Finn decided he was going to be busy as well.

"I'm going to go check on Maddox. I'll find you two later?" he said as we stepped outside, and I shook my head.

This new version we'd brought back of Neva was going to yell at me, and I wasn't in the mood for that. Maybe after I'd had a couple of Olida's hot toddies… but certainly not sober.

Finn disappeared like a coward when he knew I was going to object. Then, it was just me and Neva, and she was glaring daggers at my face.

"Quit. I didn't do anything wrong," I said, shooing her away with my hands as I took several steps back.

She followed, staying right on my heels before yanking me toward her. "You can't avoid me. You brought me here, and I have no problems following you around until you spill what's been happening."

Eyes from other fae coming and going around us stared, making me uncomfortable. "Fine, but not here."

I grabbed on to her arm and teleported us to the beach where I'd found the most comfort since being on the hidden island. The waves were rougher today, bringing driftwood and plant life onto the tan sandy beach and a stronger saltwater smell.

"Your email clearly didn't relay everything that has transpired since I left," she said first as we sat on the warm log.

"Well, I was trying to hurry," I sighed.

"Sounds like we have time now, so why don't you start from the beginning?" she suggested, but it sounded more like a demand.

I turned to meet her stare. "Did something happen to you back in LA? I know you're upset, and while I don't mind this new attitude, it's cause for concern." If one of the witches or packs touched her, I was going to kill the whole lot of them.

She sighed. "Yes and no. It wasn't easy dealing with the supernaturals. They weren't as forthcoming with information as they would have been if you'd been around. Even when I do things on my own for you, the underlying threat of you being just a call away always helped. I didn't have that this time, and they knew it."

"Oh, the threat is still there. It's just delayed for a short time," I said, cracking my knuckles as I stretched.

Neva smiled. "I knew that, but the others not so much. Nothing happened, it was just different. Then, when I didn't hear back from you… It scared me, Ms. Lucinda."

Clearly, she wasn't too far gone given she was still using "Ms."

"I really am sorry we worried you."

Neva stared out into the water. "I know you are, and that helps, but the whole situation showed me I need to speak up more. There is a lot I don't say, and life can be over in an instant. If I don't speak my mind now, I might never have the chance."

She was right about that. I should have died while trying to get to Zephyr. Now that I'd had some time to reminisce about the situation, I'd only been running on adrenaline and dark magic when Finn arrived. None of that would have gotten me very far once I was within the gates of the castle.

Though, I did find myself drawn to the thought of holding Gabriel's sword again. He hadn't owned the steel beauty when I'd been around, or never carried it, at least. I'd have remembered the power the blade exuded. I was still curious about it and wondered if the weapon could be the key to ending King Zephyr. I wouldn't let it go again if I had the chance, no matter what kind of darkness it was filled with.

Neva nudged me while I was lost in thought. "Enough about me. What happened with you? More importantly, you and Finn?" she asked.

I laughed, shrugging off my thoughts of death and dark magic. "Did you bring the popcorn? It's been one drama after another, it seems."

She grinned at me. "But you're bonded. It can't be *all* bad."

"Oh, it wasn't something I intended to do, and I'm still not sure about it, but that's a problem to handle when this is all over."

She squeezed my hand. "Tell me everything."

Neva hadn't let me leave the beach until I'd told her every detail that I could recall about what had happened while she was gone. Considering she'd been so insistent, I'd even given particulars on things she'd probably rather not have known.

The evening went by quickly once we were done catching up. When we'd arrived back at the huts, the area had been transformed into some sort of fae luau. Tiki torches lit the area, a fire pit had been made in the middle—though there was no animal roasting in it like humans often did—and the island fae were all gathered.

As the evening progressed, we drank, ate, and danced, pretending that the world around us wasn't going to shit. Well, at least most of us had. Maddox was a bit of a downer for most of the evening.

Once the healing drugs wore off, Maddox slowly became awful to be around. He was livid, murderous with his words about the king, and angry at the world. Olida threatened to drug him again if he didn't quit ruining her feast.

The following morning, our time to leave arrived much too soon. While I was eager to kill the asshole who called himself king, the night before had shown me I could have something more than the life I'd been living. The fae here didn't fear me. They had no expectations of me to be someone other than who I was.

The feeling was... unfamiliar yet comforting.

As I dressed in all black and prepared for hunting, a realization settled into me. I needed to live my life in the moment. If that meant being one person while I was on the secret island, another when I was in LA, and a monster while I hunted the king, then so be it. Maybe I didn't have to be any one thing. I could be all of them, and that would be okay.

"Ready?" Finn murmured, placing a kiss on the back of my neck as he pushed my braided hair to the side.

"I am. Are you?"

He spun me around, jerking my body against his. As my skin heated, I wished I hadn't gotten dressed so fast.

Finn kissed me until we were both breathless. "I'm ready now. Let's find the Renegades and save my sister."

I pulled my head back before he could distract me with anything else. "And kill the king."

"And kill Zephyr," he corrected, Mosi's sentiments clearly having worn off on him.

We left our hut in search of Maddox and Neva. They'd shared one of the main structures closer to Mosi and Olida in case Maddox had any issues. From what I'd seen the night before, the only issue he had left was a temperament one.

He and Neva were already outside, ready and waiting next to Mosi and Olida when we arrived. I didn't like seeing Neva's ebony curls pulled back into a tight bun and her ready for battle. She wasn't made for this kind of life, but I wasn't her mother. I wouldn't force her to stay behind.

"Everyone rested and ready to go?" Olida asked with a bright smile.

"Rested. Sated. Same thing, right?" I replied.

Maddox grunted and mumbled something under his breath that was probably best we couldn't hear.

"Should we tell Yury that we're leaving?" I asked, also curious if he should be coming with us.

Mosi shook his head. "I will visit Yury. He's settled now, and we have much to discuss. The four of you need to leave. Find the Renegades and trust your instincts. Please know we will all stand by your side when the time is right, but we only get one shot at this, Lucinda."

His mahogany eyes bored into me like he was trying to tell me something, but I had no idea what. Still, I nodded. "We're fully aware of the consequence should we fail."

Olida passed out hugs and held on to me a little longer. "You're special, Lucy. In time, you're going to see that, and I hope I'm there when you do. Please be safe and know everything we've done has been to help you," she whispered, and my chest tightened with emotions I preferred to avoid.

Instead of replying with words, I smiled briefly and distracted myself by grabbing Neva's hand and spreading my wings. She could teleport like us, but she couldn't follow our trail—that was only a fae thing. Better if one of us always had a hold on her. We didn't have time to waste trying to find each other.

"We still need to be careful, but don't forget Yury concealed your magical presence," Neva said.

He'd been such a demanding not-witch that I'd completely forgotten about that. "Thanks for the reminder. I missed you always stating the obvious."

"We see the world differently, and there's nothing wrong with that, Lucy." Neva grinned from ear to ear at my shock.

"You said 'Lucy' and you're not even trying to sway my choices. Why?" I asked.

"You're not the only one who has changed. Now, let's go before Maddox does something he shouldn't." She nodded at the fae who'd already flown off without the three of us.

"We're going to have to keep a close eye on him," I said loud enough for Finn to hear as he finished speaking with Mosi and joined us.

"Just give him time. He'll be okay. Maddox didn't know about Mosi before, so it's harder for him to trust," Finn replied.

Finn could deal with Maddox then. As long as the fae didn't cause us extra trouble, I didn't mind if he pouted, but I would step in to remind him that his actions had consequences if it was necessary.

As soon as we were all grouped together, we teleported to Finn's farm, but further out into the trees than last time. Given he'd been seen coming out of the bunker, we didn't trust it was a safe place any longer.

Slowly, we crept toward the house. I had plenty of items left in there that I hoped to still use, and this was step one to finding what remained of the Renegades.

"Do you smell that?" Finn asked as we got closer to his home. The scent of destruction permeated the stale air.

I had, but I'd been hoping it was smoke from the previous burn areas we'd seen.

Maddox began to walk faster, nearing a run, and Finn stayed with him, leaving me and Neva behind.

"Should we catch up with them?" Neva asked.

"Nope. We'll let them rush into what could be another battle first. If there are guards still waiting, I'll hide you in a tree and join them," I replied.

"I'm capable of helping, you know?"

I nodded. "But you're still innocent, and if I can help it, your hands will never spill blood."

She regarded me for a moment longer than I was comfortable with, so I stared blankly back at her, giving her no sign of emotion. We weren't going to get deep in conversation when we had no idea what waited for us ahead.

The stench of burning flesh and unnatural materials became stronger with every step we took, but I still didn't hear any shouts. We continued, picking up speed a little more with each step.

Once the farmhouse came into view, or what should have been it, my heart sank. All of the special items I'd collected while on Earth were gone. Burnt to a crisp.

Finn's jaw was tense as he stared at the rubble, Maddox nowhere in sight.

"Where is Maddox?" I asked.

Finn glanced around. "Shit. He was just right next to me."

I really didn't want to use my magic to hunt him down in case that would alert the king in some way, but having Maddox causing mayhem around the island could be just as bad.

Neva nudged me before I could make a move. "There he is."

The fae was coming out of the bunker, or at least the entrance. The shed that hid it before was also gone.

"Bunker is somewhat intact, but there's no hiding in there any longer," Maddox said, having no idea we were all thinking he'd left us.

"They burned the guards we'd killed. The bastards hadn't even taken them home for a proper burial so their families could say goodbye," Finn spat.

Neva stepped closer to him. "I'm sorry about your home."

"It's just stuff. We can replace most of it," Finn replied, but I could hear the underlying hurt in his voice. I didn't know how to comfort him as I took in the rubble that was once his home. Charred pieces of framing, metal pipes, the kitchen sink, and the stove were the only things recognizable.

As I moved around the area, searching for anything that could be salvaged, I caught sight of a paper pinned to the stove. Stepping carefully, I walked through what used to be the kitchen and snatched it.

The others waited for me, staying on the dirt as I walked back already reading the note.

Surrender yourself, Lucinda.

Every day you make me wait is another the girl is tortured.

You have the chance to end this.

Are you going to be a disappointment to everyone around you?

I didn't need a signature on the note to know who had left it. Zephyr had chosen his words carefully. Direct and to the point, just the way I preferred things. Little did he know, his words couldn't hurt me any longer. His manipulative ways didn't hold the clout they once did.

Finn held out his hand, and I gave him the note, watching all their faces as they read the words. If they thought I should surrender myself, I'd walk away. Not to give up, but to do this on my own. This was the moment that would show me how important I really was to Finn.

Maddox took three steps back, unfurled his wings, and let loose a burst of sorrowful power that nearly knocked me over, but I wasn't concerned with him. I didn't remove my sights from Finn.

He finally glanced up at me. Determination like never before set in his tense face. "We're going to kill him. I don't care who does it, but the first chance one of us has, we take it."

As much as I wanted to demand I be the one to take Zephyr's life, I had to agree. I couldn't let my desire for revenge get in the way of what needed to be done. Especially not when neither of them had asked me to turn myself in just so Ivy could be safe.

That meant more to me than even I had expected.

"I agree. It doesn't matter who strikes, just make sure you do it with everything you have," I said, watching Finn crumple the note and throw it in the rubble of his home. Though, I was already picturing myself taking possession of the sword again and slicing Zephyr's head off in the next instance.

"What now?" Neva asked.

"We find the Renegades. Isn't that what Mosi said? Aren't we supposed to be trusting him?" Maddox snapped, his fury still rolling off him in waves that couldn't be ignored.

Finn placed a hand on his shoulder. "Easy, brother. We had to know if there was anything left here. We will search for the remaining Renegades now and see what they know. Information from them could be invaluable to getting Ivy back."

"Like you even care. You have *her* now," Maddox sneered and shoved Finn away.

Finn moved swiftly, knocking Maddox to the

ground with a push of his own. "I might have Lucinda, but Ivy is still my sister. I will fight for her until my last breath. You are practically my brother. I will fight for you as well, but don't you ever doubt how much I love my family again. That's a line I won't let you cross, no matter how much you're hurting."

They glared at each other for several painfully long moments until finally Maddox gave the briefest of nods.

"Let's go, then. No time to be wasting. The sun is finally coming up, and I'd like to stay within the trees as much as possible," I said, taking no offense to Maddox's little outburst.

"The last place I'd met Edgar at when he'd been trying to get me to join him was South Island. The guards didn't use to patrol that area much since the lands are dying, but I'm not sure if that has changed in the last few days while they've hunted for us as well," Finn said after he got up.

Maddox disappeared without warning, and Finn followed with me and Neva right behind, barely catching their trail. When we reappeared, Finn had his hands on Maddox's shoulders as he bowed his head, chest heaving. Finn was doing his best, but I wasn't sure if that would be enough to keep Maddox from screwing everything up for us.

Neva began to say something, but a flutter of green caught my attention from inside the dying forest. Leaves were sparse, and seeing through the trees was easier, but the flash of color was gone before I could fully focus.

"Did you hear me?" Neva asked, but I still ignored her.

"I'll be back."

I spread my wings and took off into the trees. I had to catch whoever that was. They'd seen us, so I needed to see them.

CHAPTER 12

My wings moved swiftly until I heard a deep roar coming from Finn. Shit. I'd done it again. I was pretty sure taking off like that wasn't something I was supposed to do, but my instincts had kicked in. There was nothing I could have done to stop my actions.

As I considered slowing, I caught sight of the green again and couldn't find the will to halt my movements. Even if I'd felt the tiniest bit of guilt as I flew further away. The others would catch up and it would be fine.

Whoever was out there was fast. They darted in and out of the trees, making it impossible for me to track them or even tell if they were man or woman. The only positive part was that they weren't trying to escape, or at least it didn't seem that way to me as we moved in a big circle.

We continued to play a game of cat and mouse, moving in and out of the dying foliage. Just when I thought I was getting close, the fae disappeared and I could hear Finn right behind me.

I finally slowed so he could catch up. Clearly, after five minutes of chase, I wasn't going to get the bastard on my own.

Just as I turned around to face the direction Finn should have been coming from if I was sensing him correctly, a hard body slammed into mine and blasted me with power.

Son of a bitch. I hadn't seen that coming.

Magic surged from my hands, and I shoved the fae off me before charging at him. Something about him seemed familiar, but I couldn't place it.

Emerald gossamer wings flapped rapidly behind the newcomer as his eyes widened. Then, he held up his hands and fell to his knees just as I was about to strike him again.

"I'm so sorry, Lucinda. I didn't know it was you," he said, eyes pleading with me.

"How do you know who I am?" I asked, still ready to strike except Finn beat me to it.

My mate stormed into the clearing and crashed into the young fae. He was barely full-grown, his power strong, but fresh as if he'd just turned ten and made his first transition.

Finn pinned him down, knees holding the fae's arms and one hand pulsing magic at his throat. "Who are you?"

The fae was terrified, and something about that bothered me.

"Finn, stop," I said, surprising not only him, but myself.

Finn didn't budge. "Excuse me?"

"I know him." That wasn't a lie. I just didn't recall how I did.

Finn slowly moved, not once taking his eyes off the fae as he joined my side. "Who is he?"

The boy saved me from continuing to try to figure it out myself. "I'm Ash."

"Well, Ash. Why were you running from us?" Finn asked, a little calmer than moments before.

He pointed between the two of us. "You don't have any magical presence. I didn't know who you were, and neither did the trees."

Holy shit. He was the boy I'd seen the last time I was here, but that had only been a couple weeks ago. He was just a small child then. "How are you so big? You were maybe seven the last time I saw you," I said.

He nodded. "My power is different from yours. The trees needed me to be bigger, so that is what I became."

Finn gaped and glanced at me. "You knew he existed and didn't tell me?"

I shrugged. "To be honest, I kind of forgot about him. He was just a kid before."

Finn sighed, taking a step forward. "Can you heal the trees now that you've entered your prime years? This forest has been dying for far too long."

Ash's blue eyes met mine, bright and full of hope. "I can protect them for now, but she is the only one who can save them."

My eyes narrowed. "You said that before. What do you mean?"

Maddox and Neva joined us but stayed quiet while we waited for an answer. Ash seemed hesitant. I wasn't sure if it was because there were four of us and one of him, or another reason entirely.

Ash ran a hand over his face and into his chestnut hair. "I've been raised by these trees, but even I do not understand their reasoning. All I know is I am to help Lucinda the best I can if she needs it, but I cannot leave this island, or they will die."

"Well, unless the Renegades are here or you have information about what's going on at the castle, then I doubt you can really help us," I stated.

"The Renegades? Who are they? I've never heard of them," Ash said.

"We need to keep moving. This child can't help us," Maddox stated.

He was probably right. Ash would be powerful one day, but the trees couldn't teach him how to channel his magic. Whatever they'd been doing so far wasn't anything we could use. Plus, I had no idea how I was supposed to save the trees. Possibly by killing Zephyr?

Whatever the reasons were, I couldn't get anything accomplished by standing in a forest. "Well, Ash. Stay safe, and we'll see you around."

He reached out and stepped forward to grasp my arm. Ash's eyes closed, and power pulsed from him. "What you seek isn't here," he said as I jerked away.

"Then, where is it?" I asked. Whatever was happening in our world was bringing out all the crazy in our kind, and I wasn't going to dismiss the kid so easily.

Finn moved closer, and the young fae's power continued to grow, but it didn't feel threatening, so I stayed put and let him grab hold of me once more. He hummed and nodded several times before refocusing his eyes. "The people you need to find are on North Island."

Damn, we were just there.

Finn tried to pull me closer, but Ash didn't release my arm. "You must come back when you are free. This island will not survive without you."

I yanked my arm from his grip once more. My eyes stared directly into his. We were about the same height, but his face still held a child-like innocence to it with the roundness of his cheeks and pouty lips. "I already told you I can't heal the trees, kid."

"Just please promise to come back," he pleaded, reminding me of the fearful child he'd been the first time I met him.

"Fine, I'll be back," I said.

"Promise me," Ash insisted.

It was as if he knew I couldn't back out if I promised. Just because I didn't consider myself good, didn't mean I lacked standards.

"Fine, I promise I will be back when we've killed the king." I couldn't commit to anything else until our job was done.

"Thank you. Hurry to North Island. The trees said fae hide in the deep forest, beyond the farms, but furthest from the beaches. You will find them where you least expect." Ash released me and fluttered his wings before disappearing, once again leaving me with a cryptic message.

"Well, that was informative," I deadpanned.

"It actually was," Finn said. "North Island is the biggest within our realm, so there are plenty of places for the Renegades to hide. The forest area is miles wide and deep, but there were clues in his statement. I have a few ideas."

Finn turned to Maddox, and they began talking about landscapes and making plans for several locations to check before we took off. I glanced around, keeping my eyes out for any guards. I wasn't as worried about seeing them here as I was when we had to go back to North Island, but still. We couldn't be too careful, no matter where we were.

Neva stayed by my side, quiet and watching as well. She was taking her part in all this seriously and I wished I'd forced her outside of her comfort zone sooner.

After my third pass of searching through the trees, Finn and Maddox finally had their plan formulated.

"We are going to head into territory that isn't usually monitored, but we don't know how desperate Zephyr is. Everyone needs to be alert. Lucy, follow my trail and stay close. If you see something, don't dart off, please." Finn said the last part with exasperation, but I made no promises.

Instead, I unfurled my wings, shook my feathers out, and grabbed on to Neva. "Ready whenever you are."

He sighed, nodding to Maddox who seemed better now that we had an idea of how to find the Renegades. Whatever Mosi had meant about us knowing what we needed to do after that better be something that smacked us in the face and not be something easily ignored.

Whatever it was, I was just hoping it brought us to the castle by nightfall.

Two frustrating hours later, we were no closer to finding the Renegades than we'd been before, and we were all at each other's throats. Well, except for Neva. The poor elf was just trying to keep the peace.

"Screw this. Mosi is just some old dude with shiny wings. I'm not waiting anymore. Ivy needs us, in case you've forgotten," Maddox spat at Finn.

Finn shoved him. "She's my sister. Of *course* I haven't forgotten."

"Will you two idiots shut your damn mouths? We're going to be spotted from a mile away with as loud as you're being," I grumbled.

Maddox glared at me, pointing. "You're the reason we're in this mess."

Neva held her hands up. "You guys, this isn't—"

I laughed, cutting her off. "Right, because Ivy was doing just fine on her own before I got here. She was living her best life and still wanted to get married. Oh, wait. No, she didn't. She'd broken up with you."

Maddox snarled and lunged for me, but Finn grabbed him. "Don't you dare touch her."

"Or what?" Maddox snapped, breaking free from Finn's hold.

Neva stepped between us again. "You guys need to—"

"I can handle my own fights, *Finnigan*. Why don't you worry about yourself?" I said, moving around her to get closer to Maddox. He needed to pay for his little attitude.

Neva stomped her foot, the sound much louder than it should have been, and power I'd never sensed from her before knocked all three of us on our asses.

"I said *stop*," she snarled.

Each of us glanced at the others before giving the elf our full attention.

"That's better. Now, listen to what I've been trying to tell you. You three are being tricked. There is a powerful fae hiding in these woods."

Fury rose within me as her words fully registered. I didn't like being manipulated.

"Where?" I seethed.

"I don't know, but I sense the power. It doesn't seem to be working on me because I'm not fae. At least, that's what I think."

"And when were you going to tell us you were packing all that power?" Finn asked while I glanced around and got up.

"Nobody ever asked, and I don't like to use it, but the three of you were acting like children and left me no choice. Now, before you become bickering idiots again, follow me." Neva waltzed past us and further into the trees. She was vibrating with power, and I was intrigued.

I knew there was a reason I'd saved her. She was a closet badass.

Maddox and Finn followed at my flanks. I could sense my frustrations beginning to rise again, but I did my best to focus on Neva. Whatever trap the fae had planted in these trees was strong, and I was impressed, but it wouldn't be enough to keep us from finding them.

"There." Neva pointed to a burgundy house with cream-colored shuttered windows and a green wraparound porch.

"There what?" I asked.

"That's where the magic is coming from, and I would bet that is where the remaining Renegades are," she replied, her power lessening by the second.

This was certainly where I'd least expect them to be hiding out.

Before we could move in, the door opened, and a lady walked out with silver hair and dressed in navy just like the king's guards.

Well, that wasn't good.

CHAPTER 13

My body pulsed with magic, and my wings hardened. Finn didn't seem to recognize her, and I wasn't taking that as a good thing. I pulled a feather from my lower right wing since the left was still regrowing from the last fight and launched the pointed weapon at the fae.

Her turquoise eyes met mine, her angular face remaining taut, and she snatched the feather from the air when it was only two inches from her forehead. "That's no way to treat your fellow fae, Lucinda," she chided before flinging the feather back at me.

"Who are you?" I asked as I caught it, tucking it into my back pocket. No sense in wasting a perfectly good weapon.

The woman pushed her silver hair back, listening and watching. "Get inside. Talking out here isn't safe." Her brow scrunched as she continued to regard us. "No fae can find this place, but I didn't count on elf magic when I created the barrier."

Finn grabbed my hand as the woman turned to go back in the house. "I'm not sure this is a good idea. Whoever she is, she's powerful. Going inside doesn't seem like the wisest choice, given we have no confirmation that she's part of the Renegades."

I nodded and completely agreed with him, but we'd been out searching for what felt like forever. This was the closest we'd gotten to learning anything new. I wasn't ready to walk away just because it wasn't safe.

I turned to Neva. "What do you think, Closet Badass?"

She sighed. "First, what I did back there isn't going to happen often, so badass I am not. Second, I don't sense anything dark coming from her, so it's up to the rest of you."

Maddox glanced at the fae waiting in the doorway, then at Finn. "We have to try. For Ivy. I can't wait much longer." His voice was strained and the pain evident.

Finn ran a hand through his hair. "Damn it. What if..."

I nudged him. "You can't live life by 'what if'. That's boring." I added a wink and got a half-grin out of him.

"Fine, let's go." Finn took a step forward, keeping a hold of my hand. He seemed to like to have me close. I wasn't fond of it, but given he was on high alert, I let the display of affection slide. For now.

"Good choice," the woman muttered as she stepped into her home and held the door open for us.

We entered into the house that was not the comforting scene it portrayed from the outside. Instead of seeing a living room, kitchen, or dining room, we found a gutted building with few walls, concrete floors, reinforced windows with rods, and six other fae reclining on cots—one of which I recognized from the fight against Edgar.

Well, at least we were at the right place.

Each of them stood, waiting for the woman to speak first. She took a seat at a cheap folding table and gestured for us to do the same. "I'm Maeve. Why have you come to my home after slaughtering half of my people?"

"They were trying to kill us first, so there's that. And we thought they were Edgar's people," Finn replied as we moved closer to the chairs.

"Edgar was an imbecile, and I'd thank you for killing him if you hadn't also put a dent in my numbers," she replied, glaring at me. I'd never seen this woman before in my life, but her knowing my name and throwing hate my way warned me I'd done something unknowingly to her.

"You said 'was.' So, is Edgar really gone? I heard he likes to come back from the dead," I said, sitting down before the others and meeting her scowl with a grin.

Maeve straightened, smoothing out her aging face. "After what you did to him, I would assume that was the last we'll see of Edgar. He was a great soldier at first, but he was terrible at following orders. When you came back, he got even worse. I tried to stop him, but I was too late the day they showed up at your farm."

"We were sent here by a friend. He said you might

be able to help us get another chance at taking down the king," Maddox cut in, not surprising me when he got straight to the point.

"Who is your friend?" she asked.

Finn placed a hand on Maddox's shoulder and answered himself. "Our friend says it's important he remains unknown for now. We mean you no harm. You may not even need to directly help us, but if you have any information, we would appreciate you sharing. Zephyr took my sister, and I will get her back."

Maeve leaned back in her chair, kicking her feet up onto the table. She sighed, paying more attention to her chewed-up nails than us. "Listen, I learned long ago not to make alliances with other leaders. I might be able to help you if you're willing to do something for me, but make no assumptions about my assistance. I play for one team and that's my own. In the end, I will do whatever is bound to keep me and my people alive the longest."

Well, I'd had enough of that.

Between the aggression I'd been experiencing in the forest, her previous glares, and acting as if she knew me when I'd never seen her before, I was done playing around. She was either going to be helpful, or she wasn't.

My hand slammed down on the table, magic scorching the plastic. "No, you listen, Macy." She opened her mouth to correct my intentional mistake, but I talked over her. "Zephyr needs to die, and he will die. There is only one side for you to choose if you're playing that card. You can either help us with that or not, but I won't have anyone around whose goals don't align with ours. The Renegades almost killed the king once. You're obviously aware he's a shit leader. So, tell me how you did it."

She blinked and wrapped a piece of silver hair around her finger. "I don't think I will."

And that was when everything went to hell.

I launched myself across the table and wrapped my hands around her throat. Neva backed herself against the wall while Finn and Maddox moved to my side as the other six fae came charging toward us.

Maeve snapped her fingers and shook her head while I attempted to choke the air from her lungs. Then, she pressed her thumbs into my wrists, hitting a pressure point and adding a zap of magic for full effect.

My hands let go of their own accord and I backed up, ready to fight her however she was going to take things. Mosi was wrong. We weren't going to find any help here. We were on our own.

"Lucinda Morrow. You've changed," Maeve tittered.

My eyes narrowed. "Excuse me?"

"You're not the killer I thought you were." Then, she turned to Finn. "Your sister is as good as dead, but I will give you some advice. None of you are a risk to me."

My head shook as ire built within. I would be whoever I needed to be in order to kill Zephyr. This bitch didn't know anything about me.

Power pooled in my palm as I stared Maeve down.

I'd bide my time for the sake of Ivy, but the fae would get what she had coming to her. My gut told me she was not good people.

Neva reappeared at my side, nudging my opposite hand that I still had readied to bash Maeve's face in with. Neva nodded, almost as if giving me approval to do whatever I had planned. While I found that interesting, I didn't need her permission.

"What do you know?" Maddox asked. He and Finn stayed close to me while the other fae backed off.

"I know that King Zephyr holds a prisoner, which I assume is the woman you speak of. I know that he wants Lucinda back alive. Why? That I don't know, but I am aware that they've been growing their forces. Every able body has been taken and thrown into blue garb, forced to stay at the castle."

"That's because I killed the first half," I snarled, reminding her I was very much the killer she had doubted just moments ago.

She rolled her eyes. "Right. Anyway, the king is having issues. His body randomly moves between the midlife and after years. The magic that protects him as king is broken, and his mind is poisoned. While he is still powerful in his own right, when he is having an after-years episode, he is at his weakest."

For the first time since we started this conversation, I didn't want to punch the bitch in her face. This information was actually helpful, and I thought back to when I'd first seen him at the castle after poisoning the food and water. He'd appeared so old, but the following meeting, he was back to his same old self.

So much had been happening that I'd never questioned the changes, but it made more sense now and gave us the opening we needed. Maybe Mosi hadn't been wrong about coming here. I just wished we were getting an army out of the Renegades as well.

"How often does he change into the after-years phase?" Finn asked.

My focus stayed on Maeve, observing her turquoise eyes as they watched each of us.

Something about her wasn't adding up, and I didn't think it was only because she'd pissed me the hell off. As I paid closer attention, there was a fear within her depths that I recognized, and curiosity began to overcome the wrath.

"It's random. You need someone on the inside to tell when he's having an episode," she finally answered Finn's question, breaking eye contact.

"And do you happen to know someone on the inside?" I asked.

"Nobody who can help you," she replied, raising a challenging eyebrow toward me.

It was an interesting choice of words. I took her bait, giving her a reaction that she may or may not have expected. I let my power carry through the air, directing it to press down on her. "Are you sure about that?"

Maeve coughed as my magic wrapped around her. She kept her shoulders squared, overcoming the pain I attempted to elicit. "Very sure."

Well, at least she was strong. I'd made grown men cry with that move before. "Okay, then. You're not willing to help, and you have very little information for us. We should be on our way."

I moved to leave, assuming the others would follow, but Finn didn't budge. Instead, he asked another question.

"You said you might help us if we did something for you. What is it that you need, and what could you help us with?"

She smirked at me before answering, and my fingers itched to hurt her. "If you can get me what I want, then I will get you into the castle undetected, but once you're within the walls, you'd be on your own."

Okay, maybe she had every reason to be cocky. "How do we know you can actually do that?" I asked, turning back around.

I'd lived in the castle for five years, and even I didn't know how to enter or exit without setting off an alarm when everyone was already on high alert.

"I'll give you a blood oath," Maeve replied.

Well, shit. That was something I couldn't argue with.

"No," Maddox snarled. He'd gone ahead to the door when I wasn't watching. His eyes were dark, and the agony at having lost his fiancée was slowly breaking him down. Clearly, fairy boy didn't know what to do with those emotions. Lucky for him, that was one field I excelled in.

But first, we had business to attend to. Maddox would have to hold his shit together for just a little bit longer.

"Okay, Mary. Let's do the blood oath, and I'll get you whatever you need as long as it's within the fae realm," I said, once again calling her by something other than her own name. It was the little things that brought me the most joy.

She glared at me, reacting just the way I wanted the old bitty to. If I was under her skin, she'd slip up. Mistakes from others, as long as we were expecting them, were just what we needed in order to best Zephyr.

I wouldn't be trusting this bitch, though. Especially when she clearly said she wasn't all in for anything other than herself.

Maeve left the room, and her six renegades kept an eye on us. I smiled and waved at the lot before turning my attention back to Maddox. Finn was trying to talk to him, but he was only making things worse.

I walked over and pushed my mate out of the way. "Let me handle this. Ivy might be your sister, but you can't help Maddox."

Finn stood his ground. "Don't antagonize him, Lucy. We can't afford for him to get worse."

I flicked my hair back, glaring at him. "I can, on occasion, make things better instead of worse."

He sighed but took a few steps back. "That's not what I meant."

I ignored Finn and raised my hand to grasp Maddox's jaw, forcing him to meet my eyes. My fears, rage, darkness, and empathy all rose to the surface. I hid nothing from him, and he soaked it all in with abandon.

"How?" he asked.

"I focus on the reward," I replied, understanding he was asking how I handled it all.

"And what is that?"

I released his face while stuffing my emotions right back where they belonged. "Killing every single asshole that has wronged me."

CHAPTER 14

Maddox nodded his understanding, and I wanted to continue our conversation. He clearly needed someone to tell him it was okay to have his murderous thoughts, but Maeve was already back in the room.

She was carrying a small dagger and a bowl made from mortar that was filled with herbs normally only witches used.

"Don't you need a witch to do a blood oath?" Neva asked, suspicion lacing her words.

Maeve glared. "Not if you know what you're doing."

"How do we know if it will work?" I asked, because Neva had a point. Maeve might have had all the right stuff, but she wasn't a witch.

"It will work," Maeve snapped, seeming more defensive than necessary. Neva kept a close eye on her, and I trusted the elf to let me know if she sensed something was off. Even more so after her little show in the forest.

Finn stepped back to my side. "What is it that you want us to get for you? I'm assuming you'll be asking for our commitment in this oath, but you're not getting a drop of our blood until I know what you want is actually obtainable."

Maeve nodded and pointed at him. "You I like. You ask the right questions. What I need you to get me is the blood of a siren."

I laughed without a second thought. "You've got to be kidding me. Sirens have been dead for decades or more."

She sneered at me once again. "Just because they choose to remain unknown doesn't mean they don't live."

She had a point.

"Fine, let's say they live. How do you expect us to find them?" I asked.

Maeve shrugged. "They're somewhere within the depths of the ocean below, but figuring out where exactly is your problem, not mine."

Maddox roared, and power slammed into my back. By the time I straightened and turned around, Finn was trying but failing to restrain Maddox.

Finn's wings were wrapped around Maddox, but he was ready to tear through them in order to get to Maeve, who was apparently pissing off more than just me.

"The love of my life is being tortured, and you're being a selfish bitch. I'm about to make this *whole* situation your problem," Maddox bellowed as he broke through Finn's hold.

I stepped in. As much as I would love to see Maeve get knocked on her ass again, I also didn't want to fight our way into the castle. Maeve wasn't lying if she was willing to do a blood oath, which meant she was our best chance at getting to Ivy and possibly keeping her alive.

If we found Zephyr first, that was a different story, but I was happy to try to give everyone their happy ending if it was possible. Should Maeve be able to help us, that was plausible. Maddox needed to realize that.

Before Maddox could plow into Maeve, I built up a wave of magic deep from my core into my palms and slammed them into his chest as he tried to pass by me. My fingers gripped his shirt as he convulsed from my power, then I knocked him onto the ground.

Maddox's fists pounded into the floor as I sat on top of him, lowering myself until I had his full attention. "Listen, Maddie. I know it hurts. I've felt the kind of pain you're experiencing ten times over, but you need to learn that revenge is best served cold. You will get yours, but Maeve isn't who you're really mad at. Remember that."

He wasn't listening, and my skin was starting to burn from the heat he was putting off. So much for thinking he was nothing but a fairy boy.

I placed my hand on Maddox's chest. Instead of hurting him again, I surprised even myself and calmed him. "Breathe, Maddox. Just focus on that one task."

Within a few moments, he was back in control and I got up, turning to Finn. "You got this?"

There was a shine in his eye I wasn't familiar with, but he nodded, and that was all that mattered as I hauled Maddox up with me, shoving him out the door.

He went willingly and headed for the trees, but I stopped him. "We don't know how Maeve's wards on this place work. I wouldn't get too far if I was you."

He grumbled, but still came back to where I stood just beyond the porch. "I can't let Ivy stay there another day."

"You're going to have to figure your shit out. I want Zephyr dead as much as you want Ivy back, but I've been in this world long enough to know that brute force isn't always the best play. Given what we've learned and the things Mosi *didn't* say, I have a feeling this is only the beginning of our frustrations."

"That's easy for you to say. You don't care about anything," he snapped.

My fingers tapped on my thighs. I hadn't even opened up to Finn like this, but something about Maddox's pain was making me want to help him. The words came out before I could think twice.

"That's a lie. I care too much. I cared about my parents. I cared about the animals in my neighborhood. Even Zephyr and that damn shifter. Then, there was Neva. She was the first person who saw me for what I really was. I cared about all of those people, and most of them let me down. So, I learned how to put those kinds of emotions aside. Tuck them away, never to be thought of again."

"And now?" he asked.

"And now, well, we're not talking about me. This is about you. Get your shit together like a big boy, or the only thing you're going to do is get Ivy killed before I do. Unleash whatever is inside you, but make sure you do it on those who deserve it, at the right time. Acting like an idiot toward the ones trying to help you won't get you anything."

"How do I know who deserves it and when it's the right time? I was pretty sure Maeve had it coming."

I grinned. "You're right, but it wasn't the right time. As much as I enjoyed antagonizing her in there, we still need something from her. Mosi wouldn't have sent us here otherwise," I replied.

He grunted. "Mosi. I don't like that fae."

"You don't like that he isn't bloodthirsty like the two of us. I thought I didn't like him at first, but it's more that he hasn't exactly proven we can trust him. I don't think he's a bad fae. I'm more worried that what he deems good doesn't align with what is right."

Even if I'd changed, I still believed in my theory that right didn't always mean good, but I was learning patience to see what cards others had up their sleeves.

"I never expected you'd be the person to get me to see some sort of reason," Maddox said.

I laughed. "Yeah, neither did I. Pain and grief aren't easy to deal with, but you can't let them rule your life. You have to find a way to keep moving in the right direction."

That was something I hadn't done in a long time, but I was getting there.

Maddox nodded. "Thank you for telling me what you did. It doesn't exactly make me feel better, but I think I understand."

I placed a hand on his shoulder. "I hope you never actually understand, Maddie." Then, I went back inside. He would be okay. As long as he saved that anger for Zephyr.

We all had to do things we didn't like. It was a part of life, and the quicker he accepted that, the quicker we could get back inside the castle.

Maeve and her men were gone by the time I entered, but Finn and Neva were in deep conversation. "What did I miss?" I asked when I joined them.

"Neva completed the blood oath with Maeve," Finn answered.

I pursed my lips. "Didn't you need all of us present for that?"

Neva shook her head. "Technically, I'm the only one linked to the commitment, but I didn't think it much mattered. We're all in this together."

The elf's honey eyes met mine. There was a trust there I didn't deserve. Not after how I'd treated her for so long, but I was glad she'd thought differently of our relationship even when I'd been an asshole.

"So, what next?" I asked.

"We need to find the blood of a siren. Neva was just explaining to me how we can breathe underwater," Finn said dryly.

I chuckled. "Is someone afraid of the ocean?"

His silver eyes narrowed at me. "We have no clue what's down there. I'm just being cautious."

I pinched his chin between my fingers. "You're so cute when you're cautious." Letting go, I turned to Neva. "So, how are we supposed to find a siren without scuba gear or dying?"

"We need to find reeds that grow on the sea floor," she replied as Maddox walked in.

He stood by Finn, and they had some weird bromance moment that I ignored as Neva answered me.

"Well, one of you is going to have to swim down there and get us some. Who can hold their breath the longest?"

"I'll do it," Finn said without hesitation. My chest constricted at the thought of him swimming to the bottom of the ocean where supernatural sea creatures apparently lived, but I brushed the fear aside and nodded.

"I'm assuming we can teleport out of here at least?" I asked.

"We should be able to," Neva answered.

Maddox held his hand up. "Wait a minute. What happened to Maeve and her people?"

"Neva confirmed the blood oath," Finn said for the second time, and I coughed.

"Closet badass."

"Then, they left. Said they'd give us time to figure out our plan, but they'd be waiting and not to make it long. Gave us twenty-four hours to come back, or the deal would be dead. Maeve seems to be afraid that if we found her, so can Zephyr," Finn continued without missing a beat, adding even more information than before.

Maddox grumbled, and I kicked him as I turned for the door. "Come on. We know what we need to do. Time to head for the ocean."

All four of us left the house, and I wondered where Maeve and the six others would have hidden. I couldn't sense them anywhere, but I also wasn't searching terribly hard. I still didn't want to use my magic unless I had to. We didn't exactly know how Yury's block on us worked.

My concern was it only concealed us as fae, but not the use of our magic—something we should have asked him before we left, but I'd felt distracted and eager to go. A mistake I wouldn't repeat again once we got back.

As much as I wanted to get back to the castle, getting in a battle with the guards wasn't going to be the best way to do that.

Once we were all together outside, we walked about a hundred yards from the house at Neva's request, and Maddox led the teleport. We were still on North Island, ending up on a remote beach.

"This is as far from any farm as we can get. Probably the best place to go in the water, given we have no idea where we're going when we get underneath," Maddox said.

"We'll be right back," Finn said to the others as he pulled me aside.

We were headed toward the trees. "I don't think a quicky is appropriate right now, Finnegan. They'd still hear us."

He shook his head at me. "That's not what we're doing."

At least some things hadn't changed. I could still annoy him with my delightful humor.

"I just wanted to know what happened with Maddox without putting him on the spot. What did you say to him?" he asked.

I shrugged. "I just told him some stuff that made him see reason. He's a little better at that than you are, by the way."

"What did you say exactly?" he pushed.

"I don't remember. I wasn't expecting to have to repeat it. Something about revenge best served cold and he needed to have some patience, or he was going to get Ivy killed."

Finn's eyes widened. "And he took that well?"

"Eh. Better than you would have." I patted his cheek with a wink.

He grasped my hand and pulled me flush against his body. "Thank you for doing that. I know it's not something you'd normally do."

Gods, he was sexy when he got handsy.

"Did I say you could touch me like that?" I teased softly as I held on just as tightly.

Finn seemed to take my words as a challenge, and the bond between us flared to life. He moved his hands up my arms and tangled his fingers into my hair. "The bond… it's been too long since I touched you. I need to remind you that you're mine, Lucinda. That *this* isn't worth giving up."

His lips crashed down on mine in a bruising kiss, and my own hands grabbed on to him as our tongues tangled. My body heated until it became hard to breathe. I was no stranger to sexual desires, but even I couldn't deny, nothing before had ever felt like it did when I was with Finn like this.

My skin began to tingle, then my bones ached with need only he could satisfy. My heart raced and breathing became a chore instead of natural. Even though I wasn't sure about the bond, the power it elicited was easy to get lost in.

Finn kept one hand in my hair and showed off his strength by using the other to cup my ass and lift my feet off the ground.

I responded by wrapping my legs around his waist, thinking maybe he'd had second thoughts about a quicky on the beach. He turned us so that my back was pressed against a tree, the bark digging into my shoulders, but there was nothing that could distract me from the way our emotions flowed freely between us.

Finn was pulsing with a passion that was tinted with rage, which seemed fitting, considering our relationship so far. Even before there was a bond, there was desire mixed with fury from our very first meeting. Something I'd wanted to ignore and was currently glad I hadn't.

His grip on my hair tightened as he tilted my head back, trailing kisses across my jaw and then down my neck. His teeth scraped over my shoulder as he loosened his hold. "Do you understand, Lucinda? Mine."

His eyes were mostly charcoal by that point, and I couldn't disagree with him, even if a part of me still wanted to. That part grew smaller and smaller with every interaction.

I glanced over his shoulder and caught Neva casting glances our way. As much as I wanted to take advantage of Finn's alpha mood, because it was hot as hell, I knew we had work to do.

I slid down his body and rested my hand on his chest. "How about you go get those reeds, and we can all go for a swim together? Some of us need to cool off."

His forehead pressed against mine, the bond still raging between us. "That's probably a good idea."

Neva cleared her throat, having snuck up on us. "Um, Ms. Lucinda? Maddox is gone."

I turned my head toward her, still pressed against Finn. "And where did he go?"

"He didn't want to wait any longer. He said he would find the reeds and be right back."

"Shit." Finn gently pushed away from me and ran for the water. Before I could say anything, he was already diving in.

Neva eyed me but didn't say anything.

I grabbed her elbow, pulling her with me as I walked closer to the shoreline. "I don't think so. No more acting all prim and proper. Not after what I saw in the forest. No more miss or mister. Just be yourself, Neva. There's nothing wrong with that."

She sighed. "Old habits are hard to break, but if I'm being honest, you and I, we're not so different. Besides the fact I've lived for hundreds of years."

I laughed until my sides ached as I watched the

water, looking for signs of Finn or Maddox. "How do you figure?"

Neva kept her gaze on the horizon as well when she spoke in a somber voice. "I told you I had a family, but I was alone the day you found me, because I'd left them long before that."

"Why?" I asked.

"Because I hurt them."

I glanced at her, but she still wouldn't look my way. "Neva, you couldn't hurt a fly. I don't believe it."

She snorted, something very unlike her. "The closet badass you saw? She used to come out a lot more. I never used my power to hurt people without just cause, but one day I did. I made the wrong decision and people died."

I turned her toward me. "What happened to you?"

Her honey eyes held tears, and my chest constricted with rage at her unease.

"Nothing happened to me. I was perfectly fine, but I can't say the same for those around me. Innocent people were hurt, because I made a bad call. I thought I was saving our village, but instead, I demolished it."

"You made a mistake, Neva," I said, not knowing how to comfort her.

"A mistake that killed people, Lucinda. It's why I don't use my power like I could. I can't chance hurting another innocent person." She sniffled and moved away from me.

I yanked her back. "Don't do that. Don't pull away from me just when you show me the real you. I've always been honest with you, and the Neva I've seen over the last two days is the one I prefer. Mistakes happen and, while they have consequences, we have to learn to live with them. I've made plenty of my own, and I've done my best to right them in my own ways. You need to learn how to do the same. I won't let you lose your true self to your past."

Gods, not having the cursed darkness within me had freed my emotions in unexpected ways. Most of which I wasn't fond of, but if this new me could help Neva, then I was more than okay with that.

Neva reached to hug me and, for the first time ever, I hugged her back.

"You're going to be okay, I promise," I said, knowing full well I would risk my life to make sure that was one promise I never broke.

CHAPTER 15

*A*fter another few moments, Neva and I took a pause on the heavy conversations. I wanted to know more about what Finn and Maddox were supposed to be doing.

"How hard are these reeds to find?" I asked while watching the waves for one of their heads to pop up.

"I don't know. It's just something I learned about in a book I read once," she replied casually.

My eyes widened. "A book? You don't even know for sure if this will work?"

"Nothing is ever for sure, Lucy, but it is the best option. Unless you have another idea."

Of course, I didn't, or I would have already been doing it and she knew it. Damn elf.

"So, what else did this book say, and where did you read it?" I asked. I needed some sort of conversation to be happening while we waited, or I was going to be diving into the water after them.

We walked closer to the water line, Neva peering

into the depths just as much as I was. "Well, I worked for the council for a while, and they have this—"

"You what?" I interrupted. "How come you never told me this?"

She shrugged. "You never asked."

I grimaced. She was absolutely right. I might have missed the voice inside me, but without it, I'd also been able to pay attention to more things around me, which wasn't a bad thing. Or at least I hoped it wasn't.

"Tell me more about the book, but I'll also want to know about the council. I've never met anyone who has worked for them before," I said.

The supernatural council was the most secretive yet effective form of ruling I'd ever known. They were unknown, yet feared, but that didn't always stop idiots from thinking they could best the council. Those who were stupid enough to try often became well acquainted with the ruthless hunters sent after those who broke the rules. I enjoyed toeing the line, but even I knew better than to land myself on their radar. I was actually surprised Zephyr hadn't received a visit yet, but he hadn't technically broken any of the founding supernatural laws.

He hadn't revealed our kind to the humans. He hadn't tortured humans, only his own people. But even then, he didn't lay a hand on them. Burning lands and cutting off water supply wasn't against the laws. It was just a dick move.

There were other laws that were broken down further, but the two main ones were only keeping our secret and not abusing the humans. Zephyr just happened to get lucky and have his own realm full of fae to unleash his horrors on.

Neva sighed. "It was nearly a century ago that I worked for them. Before I, you know, did what I did. Anyway, I was a research assistant. When they didn't need me for projects, I read for fun."

I grinned, because I could absolutely picture her curled in the corner of a library, surrounded by stacks of books and in her element.

"Your kind always fascinated me, because you're the only one with a separate world. The witches and elves, no matter how similar our magic is, could never replicate that kind of power." She waved her hand around us. "My pocket realm could never compare to what the fae have created. I wanted to know more about it. The books didn't speak of your magic in detail, but they did talk about the creation of your realm quite a bit."

"Can you still get access to any of it?" I asked, curious about our history and why none of those books were within the castle. Or maybe they were. I certainly had never taken the time to look for them.

"No. When you work for the council, you live with them. I was brought in through a portal, and never left the walls of their compound until I was ready to be done. Then, I went home through another portal, having no clue where I'd been. I would have assumed the council would strip my memories, but they don't seem to fear a retaliation."

Interesting. This was the most I'd ever heard about them. Not that it really mattered. We wouldn't get their help with Zephyr. But I still wanted to know more about the life within our waters.

"What did the books say about the waters and creatures that apparently live in our realm?" I asked.

Neva tensed, and I followed her gaze out into the waters. Shit, for a few minutes, I'd forgotten we were waiting on Finn and Maddox. Supernaturals could hold their breaths longer than humans, but it was bordering on too long.

"Did you see something?" I asked while looking as well.

She paused, then pointed to our left. "There."

I saw Maddox's head, and he was dragging Finn with him, barely keeping above water. Without hesitation, I ran into the incoming waves and swam for them. The surfs pushed me further out with a vengeance, and I understood quickly why Maddox was struggling.

The water was not happy being disturbed.

"He got stung by something with creepy tentacles," Maddox groaned with the effort to keep his head above water.

I grabbed on to one of Finn's arms, and we worked together against the water. Something brushed against my leg, and I kicked my foot even harder, making contact without saying anything. All I could focus on was getting Finn back to the shore.

Whatever had been there didn't come back and we finally made it to the sand. Finn had a gash on his arm that was oozing black.

"What the hell happened down there?" I snarled as

Neva bent down to inspect the wound and check Finn's vitals.

He was my mate. I was bonded with him. But I was frozen. Just like before when the five guards had been attacking him, I lost all sense of rationale. I couldn't focus on the thought that he was maybe dying from some poisonous sea creature. Instead, I channeled my emotions into Maddox and grabbed on to his neck when he didn't answer.

"Maddox can't answer you if you're choking him," Neva reminded me.

"Well, he wasn't doing it anyway. At least this way I feel better." Maddox's eyes widened when I squeezed tighter.

"Lucy, drop him." Neva was getting bossy as the days passed, and I couldn't decide if I was proud as hell or irritated by it.

Instead of continuing to distract her from helping Finn, I did what she said, and Maddox crumpled to the ground, gasping for air.

I bent down, my knees grazing the sand, and I got in his face. "I will only ask one more time. What happened to Finn?"

"I already had the reeds. I was on my way back. He was just out of reach above me when twenty-foot-long tentacles came out of nowhere. They reached for both of us, but I managed to dodge out of the way. When one of them struck Finn, a thundering clap sound echoed around us and we were pushed further out into the water. By the time I caught up to him, he was already unconscious."

I turned back to Neva and Finn, unsure what to do with Maddox's information. It hadn't made my anxiety any better. "Is he okay?"

The paleness of her normally umber face was only making matters worse. "I don't know. Without knowing what struck him, I'm not sure what to do. I think it was a form of octopus from Maddox's description, but the dark ooze coming from the wound makes me think squid."

"What's the difference? How do we heal him?" I demanded.

"There's a huge difference. If it's an octopus, we probably have to cut off his arm before the poison gets into his blood stream, if it's not already too late. If it's squid, then one of us could suck the poison out, but risk infecting ourselves, or you could pee on him. Urine has the best chance at neutralizing the toxins before they spread, but only if we hurry."

"Crazy little elf, come again? Those are literally the worst options ever." My jeans were literally glued to me from the saltwater. I could get them off if I wanted to with magic, but really? Peeing on him? I wasn't a dog. I would not mark him, but if I had to, I'd go all vampire on Finn to save him.

"There were two longer, skinnier tentacles, so I think you're right with the squid thought, Neva," Maddox said as he crawled closer to his friend.

I moved through the sand, getting near enough to grab hold of Finn's arm. My hands warmed as I touched him, and more ooze dumped out of the wound. "What the hell was that?" I screeched as I tossed his arm back down, afraid I'd made things worse.

Finn's body began to shake, and his eyes opened wide as he turned toward me. "Help," he croaked, then he passed out again.

What in the actual hell was happening?

"Grab on to him again, Lucinda," Neva demanded.

"Not happening. Did you see what just happened?" I replied, inching back even further.

Her arm moved faster than I expected, and she latched on to me. "I think your bond can help him. I don't actually think the pee suggestion will work at this point, and we can't risk both of you dying if you swallow the poison. So, hold his arm for another minute. At this point, it can't hurt."

"Fine, but if he dies, I can't promise you won't be next."

She nodded as both she and Maddox held Finn down so he couldn't hit himself or one of us if his body began convulsing again. Once they were in place, I put one hand on his chest and the other wrapped around his arm just above the wound.

Like before, more ooze came out. Then, he began screaming. His pain was becoming mine, and I wanted to cry for the first time since I was a child, which pissed me right the hell off. I didn't cry. I didn't ever care this much. Gods, I so did not like this bond.

"Come on, Finn. Fight whatever is in you," I snarled, holding on tight enough that I was certain my fingers would leave marks when I released him.

Another half-minute later, the dark ooze turned into

blood, and Neva moved to cover the gash with a scrap piece of her shirt she'd torn off at the bottom. Once the wound was bandaged, I let go and sat in the sand, still not convinced Finn was okay.

"I don't know how you did it, but it worked," Neva said as she stood.

I scoffed. "How do you know?"

"If he was stung by some kind of squid, that liquid seeping into the sand would have traveled through his bloodstream and went for his heart. It would have killed him, but somehow, you were able to reverse its direction. You saved his life."

Maddox fell back into the sand and groaned. "We can't go back in those waters. I won't do that again."

Well, at least he wasn't pissed off at the world for the moment.

Finn began coughing, and I rolled him over, making sure to keep clear of the crap that had already nearly disappeared into the ground. "Come on, Finnegan. Just breathe. Like you always tell me."

My hand slammed into his back, probably harder than was helpful, but I was furious with him for scaring me so much. It didn't matter that it wasn't his fault he got hurt. It *was* his fault I was starting to care so damn much.

Finn finally sat up on his own. "I thought I was dead." His eyes met mine, the charcoal coloring prominent.

"You weren't dead, but I would have killed you again myself if you had been," I replied, standing up and then giving him a hand to do the same.

When I pulled him up, he didn't let go of my hold and brought me closer instead. I thought he was going to kiss me, and I went into panic mode. My hand itched to hit him, and I didn't know what was wrong with me. I more than enjoyed kissing Finn, but in front of other people and right after he almost died, it was too much for me. I was on bond overload.

Thankfully, he seemed to sense that and gave me some space but didn't let go of me.

"We can't go back in there. We'll die and then who is going to save Ivy? There's a reason that bitch didn't get the siren blood herself. This is a suicide mission," Maddox said, his hate for the world back where it had been before he dived into the ocean.

"We just need to stay in open waters as much as possible and avoid the sea floor. You must have been close to the rocks. Nothing good lives in the rocks," Neva said.

"Well, where do the sirens live?" I asked.

"In caves," she replied.

I laughed. "Isn't that the same thing?"

She shrugged. "Depends on what the caves are made from."

"I don't like it. It's too dangerous, and if I'm going to die, it's going to be saving Ivy, not helping some unknown fae who hides in the forest like a coward while other people fight her battles," Maddox said, making a very valid point.

"I hate to say it, but I agree with fairy boy. But I also know unless we get help in the form of an army, we won't all make it through those castle walls. It's a shit situation," I added.

Finn was the only one who hadn't said anything yet, and we all looked at him. He stared off into the ocean, giving no inclination as to what he was thinking until he spoke.

"Maddox, Ivy is my sister. She is my flesh and blood. I would die for her. You might be angry, but you know those things to be true. I was at the castle with Lucinda the day she tried to get in. They almost killed her then, and they've only had more time to prepare since. We need Maeve's help. We have to find the sirens. There is no other choice."

"What about Mosi and his warriors? They helped before, can't they do so again?" Neva asked.

Finn shook his head. "Mosi is very particular about when his help will come. His path doesn't cross with ours right now."

"Are you sure about that? Or is he just choosing to wait until it's convenient for him?" Maddox protested, but Finn ignored him, taking the handful of reeds I hadn't noticed sticking out of the side pocket of Maddox's pants.

"I'm going in that water. Anyone is welcome to join me, but I won't hold it against you if you don't," Finn said as he stuck one of the reeds into his mouth and handed the rest to Neva.

Well, I wasn't one to back down from a challenge.

Maddox and Neva joined us. Though, I would have been okay if they stayed behind. It would probably be better if there were less of us in the water. Then again, sticking together could also be safer in case the guards happened to find them on the beach.

"So, how do these reeds work?" I asked Neva, remembering we'd never finished our earlier conversation about what might exist in the open seas.

"When you're in the water, you should just have to blow in them like a snorkel," she answered.

Well, that seemed too easy. The reeds were about half an inch thick and open at both ends like a straw. I wasn't sure how that was going to prevent water from going into our lungs, but I was game to see how it played out.

Finn moved into the ocean first, and I followed with Neva and Maddox right behind us. I kept the reed in my hand until we were several yards out and the sand was no longer at our feet. The water was crystal clear, something I hadn't noticed before when I was more concerned with Finn possibly being dead.

Small white fish in large schools swam around us at the surface. They reminded me of puppies, so I reached out, surprised when they let me touch them. We continued until it was time to use the reeds. I stuck mine in first and turned to face the others.

Each of them had the sticks in their mouths when we ducked all the way underneath the surface, but nobody seemed like they were breathing. Since Neva had said they could be used like snorkels, I pinched my nose and breathed deep, in and out. Nothing but air came back in. Then, I noticed a bubble forming at the tip of the reed.

Deciding to do it again, this time I focused more on the breathing out. With three big pushes, I created a bubble large enough that it formed all the way around my face.

The others had already begun to follow my lead and, within another minute, we all looked like idiots with bubbles around our heads, but I no longer had to hold my nose while I inhaled.

"Can you guys breathe?" I asked, keeping the reed in my mouth like a cigarette.

Finn's eyes pinched together as he swam closer. "What?"

It looked like he was yelling, and the word was barely audible. Apparently, talking wasn't something this sort of magic reed was made for.

Finn pulled the reed from his mouth, and his bubble

started to dissipate. He recovered and had it back in place quickly.

"Keep the reeds in your mouth and just follow me," I yelled and continued swimming. I decided to take the lead. I needed to do something productive before I killed someone.

Using my arms and legs, I swam until I realized I was making this harder on myself. My wings extended, and I hardened the feathers, using the solid surface to help propel me forward like flippers. My speed was faster than the others, so I slowed and waited for them to catch up.

Finn had his wings out, but Maddox's weren't as solid as ours and Neva didn't have any, so it wasn't going to work while trying to stay together.

"I'm going to take Neva, and Finn can take Maddox," I yelled, while using my hands to signal my plan, hoping they understood as I latched on to the elf.

She didn't fight me, so I assumed they'd at least understood what I was doing. The waters stayed clear as we circled around to face the islands. The sun cut through and allowed decent visibility, but I assumed that would only last until we were forced to head deeper under the water.

Neva had mentioned the creatures she read about. The probability that we'd come upon something sinister like Finn and Maddox already had seemed high, making me extra cautious. I might be a badass on land, but I wasn't an idiot. Being down here was an entirely different scenario, and something told me that a siren wasn't just going to pop out and willingly offer up her blood.

I continued forward, ignoring the chill along my arms as we swam deeper and the water cooled. We followed around the outer edge of the island during our descent, passing colorful coral, starfish, and even a sea turtle. None of that held my attention as we came closer to massive groupings of seaweed.

Beyond that were massive rock formations, but visibility was shit beyond another twenty or so feet as the sun's light didn't reach under the island's shelf.

Bringing my attention back to the seaweed, I knew anything could be hiding within the floating vines and we would likely have no idea until it was too late. I called on my magic as I slowed, not wanting to make any sudden movements. My hold on Neva tightened as a shimmer caught my attention. I tried to focus on it, but the water started to swirl and whipped around us, making visibility nearly impossible.

I lashed out, but my magic didn't travel the same under water. Instead of going where I wanted, the waves pushed it around, and we ended up surrounded by bubbles that began to spin until I felt like we were in a cyclone.

Neva stayed within my grasp, but I couldn't see her, and I had no idea where Finn and Maddox were. Best case, they were right below us or somewhere that they could keep an eye on us and figure out what the hell was happening.

The pull became severe, and the reed ripped from my mouth. Before I closed my lips, I sucked in a shit-ton of saltwater and began choking. Neva was clawing her way up my body, and I saw her reed was also gone. Her face was already turning red, and she was beginning to panic.

The only thing I could think to do was practically kiss her and give her my breath. Before I could really freak her out, we were pulled apart and yanked into the murky waters I'd been trying to avoid. My head hit something hard, making me nearly lose consciousness as my vision wavered. When I opened my eyes again, I was staring up at a rock ceiling, breathing normally and with no water around us.

What the hell?

Neva, Finn, and Maddox were next to me, just coming to as well. When I sat up, another flash of silver caught my eye and I tensed. We definitely hadn't ended up here on our own, and we weren't alone.

"Who are you?" I asked, staring into the shadows where I saw the flicker.

"The better question is what are you doing in my home?" a woman's voice replied.

I rolled my eyes. "I can't answer that. We certainly didn't come here willingly."

She stepped from the shadows. Sleek white hair trailed down her chest and back, ending at her waist. Bright aqua eyes glared at me, and her skin was nearly translucent. Whoever she was, she clearly didn't get out of her hidey-hole very often. Even so, she was stunning in her own way.

"Are you telling me someone dropped you in the waters and forced you to swim closer to the rocks instead of back to shore?" she asked, taking another step closer and revealing a skintight black dress with two slits going all the way up her thighs.

"No, but someone did force us into this cave, which I assume is your home," I replied as I stood up, not willing to show any fear of the unknown supernatural.

She got in my face. "Everything within the water is my home. Now, tell me. Who are you, and why should I not kill you for disrupting my day?"

I glanced back at Neva. "Did your books happen to mention anything about this psycho?"

Before the elf could answer, I was smacked in the face. The hit had a bite to it that made my jaw rattle. I moved to retaliate, but Neva was suddenly standing between me and the other woman.

"I believe this is the sea queen, Lucinda. *Please,* be careful," she begged.

The woman withdrew from my personal space and narrowed her eyes at me. "Lucinda? Lucinda Morrow?"

I rubbed my cheek, really wanting to ignore Neva's advice. "The one and only."

"You killed my Edgar," she said without emotion.

Her Edgar? Oh gods, the rumors Finn had mentioned before about how Edgar kept coming back to life were true. Just the details were slightly off. Mermaids and witches had nothing to do with it.

"In all fairness, he tried to kill me first. Well, at least the second time around," I replied.

She nodded and relaxed even more, completely confusing me. "I am Alana, Queen of the Sea. Edgar is my mate. While he has strayed in his purpose, he meant well with his intentions."

"You were mated to him?" I gaped. I was having a hard time picturing the gruff fae being the perfect match for the flawless queen. Then again, me and Finn were complete opposites in our beliefs, so I had no room to judge.

"Yes, he has been mine for only a decade and was supposed to have joined me long ago to live in the sea, but my Edgar is easily distracted."

"Why didn't you just go get his ass and make him stay in the water? Sure would have made things easier on us," I said.

She bristled at my words. "Going above leaves my people vulnerable and lessens my power. I have only been on land twice during my ruling. The first time was when Edgar's soul called to me, and the second was when you killed him seven years ago." Alana glared at me, clearly not amused with my past actions.

"How did you save him?" Neva asked.

"When he died, his soul came to me. All of those who belong to the ocean come to me when their time has ended. I didn't expect Edgar's soul, because he is not of the sea, but our bonding must have given us the connection to make sure I didn't lose him before his time. I kept his soul contained, found his body, and shoved him back inside once I healed his wounds."

My face scrunched. "Shoved him inside, huh? I bet that was a pleasant experience for both of you."

"Love does not come without sacrifice, Lucinda," she replied with a huff.

"Did you bring him back again this last time?" Finn asked, moving to join us with Maddox right behind him.

Alana shook her head. "I have his soul, but he's in a timeout for not listening to me."

I laughed and she glared at me. "Come on. He's a grown-ass man and you have him in a timeout that includes keeping him dead. That is hilarious."

"Nothing about death is funny," she said solemnly.

"Well, the last time I saw him, he wasn't exactly whole. How are you going to shove his soul back inside without a body?" I asked, because it certainly sounded like she was going to try.

She shrugged. "I didn't say I was going to bring him back as a fae this time. He's had his time above ground. It's time for him to be by my side where he belongs. Well, one day it will be. Now, enough about that. I need to know something." She reached for my hand, but I yanked it back.

"I don't think so, lady. I don't care what you're the queen of. There's nothing you need to know about me. We didn't come here to see you."

"That doesn't very much matter now. I have you here, and I'm not going to let you leave until I'm ready," Alana snarled, showing off pointed teeth I hadn't noticed yet, or she'd just made them appear. Likely the latter.

Maddox stormed forward and bumped me out of the way. "Listen, lady. My fiancée needs us to get to her, and I'm not in the mood to waste time. Put us back in the water. We will get what we need and leave. We are not a threat to you or your ocean."

Maddox was practically spitting in her face, he'd gotten so close, but instead of being mad, Alana's face softened. She placed a hand on his chest. "Your heart hurts like mine does. I miss my Edgar as well. What is it that you need to get your love back?"

"We need the blood of a siren," Maddox answered through gritted teeth, barely keeping his shit together, but whatever was happening, he was reaching the sea queen on a level the rest of us couldn't.

She nodded and closed her eyes. Then, she reopened them and stared at me while moving away from Maddox. Well, maybe I was wrong.

"What are your intentions, Lucinda?" she asked.

"I'm going to kill Zephyr."

"What about his fiancée? Will you help him?" Alana asked.

I hesitated and that was answer enough for all of them. I hated that I did so, but Ivy knew, and she had even told me. Zephyr needed to die. I couldn't do both, but I would at least give Ivy the best chance I could at survival.

"I might not be able to help, but Maddox and Finn will. We also have a witch on standby to assist," I finally answered after trying to ignore her disapproving gaze.

Alana nodded. "Right, but will that be enough?"

I wasn't sure if I was supposed to answer that, so I didn't. I had enough shit on my plate. I wasn't going to get into anything with the sea queen that didn't actually concern her. It would be a waste of both of our times.

Finn stepped to my side. "None of that matters if we can't get what we need. Just let us go, so we can find the sirens. We are not a threat to you."

"Well, you might have a hard time with that."

"And why is that?" Finn asked.

"Because all of the sirens are dead."

CHAPTER 17

*M*aeve must have known this. After the poisonous squid and crazy sea queen, I had no doubts that Maeve had sent us into the waters hoping we'd die, so she wouldn't have to follow through on the blood oath. She'd probably already lost dozens of fae trying to find the sirens. Her "help" and blood oath were nothing more than a ploy.

"What do you mean they're dead? *All* of them?" Maddox asked, inching closer to Alana once more.

She frowned, something that seemed awkward on her angular face. "I'm afraid so. A darkness swept through our waters and killed many of our kind. The sirens, selkies, and water dragons were among the biggest casualties, and only very few of the dragons remain. The other two were eradicated. When their souls came to me all at once, I nearly died myself. I believe I was the true target, but Edgar saved me. It was when I first met him."

Hmm, I wondered if Edgar had actually been the

one to send the darkness through the waters. He'd obviously been messing with some powerful magic throughout the years if he'd almost been able to kill Zephyr.

Alana backed up, spun on her three-inch heels, and walked into the shadows.

"Where is she going?" I asked in case I'd missed something during my musings.

"No idea, but she better be quick about whatever she's doing, or I'm out of here," Maddox grumbled.

Finn placed a hand on his shoulder. "Easy, brother. We're almost done. By nightfall, we will be entering the castle."

Maddox shrugged him off. "At least one of us will be."

I glanced at Neva. "Any thoughts? You've been awfully quiet over there."

"The sea queen isn't a bad person. We can trust her, but I don't know how she will be able to help us."

I raised a brow. "And why is that?"

"Well, she said they're all dead. How do we get the blood of someone who no longer lives?"

Alana glided back into the cavernous area like the queen she called herself. "Dead does not mean gone, my dear." Alana held a ceramic bottle in her hand and shook it. "This is the blood of a siren. Those of the water do not perish without leaving behind something that will help the future."

"So, everyone here is an organ donor?" I asked.

Finn glared at me, silently telling me to shut the hell up.

"Do you want the blood or not?" the queen snapped, not appreciating my curiosity.

Maddox strode over and took it. "We do. Now, can we get out of here?"

Alana offered him a kind smile. "I hope you save her. Love is always worth fighting for."

With those words, Finn's eyes softened toward me, and I wondered what thoughts the queen's words triggered for him. We might be bonded, but we certainly didn't love each other. I was pretty sure I wasn't capable of that particular emotion any longer. Not after all I had been through.

I could care for people, but my heart was closed for business. The only part of me that gave a damn about anything was my head. Those feelings I allowed myself were easy to shut off with my mind, but if I ever let them into my heart... that wasn't something I cared to experience again.

Alana's white hair glowed with magic as she spoke next. "I will get you back to the surface, but you have to make me a vow."

"And what is that?" Finn asked.

"None of you will come or send anyone for Edgar when I decide it is his time to live again. He won't walk your lands, and you will not come into my waters with ill intentions. Edgar is mine, and I will protect him with my life. No one will win against me if they try to harm my mate."

"Fair enough. You keep him from trying to kill me or innocent people, and you won't ever see us again," I replied.

Alana smirked. "Well, I don't know about that last part, but I will take your words as your vow to leave my mate be." She snapped her fingers, and a silver trident appeared in her palm. A wave of power settled over the cave, and I reached for Finn and Neva as Maddox stepped closer.

Water that hadn't been present seconds before began to swirl around us, causing my iridescent locks to wrap around my face until I couldn't see any longer. Neva tightened her grip on my arm, and I did the same to Finn. I had no idea what to expect, but it certainly wasn't warmth and comfort to envelop me.

A floating sensation took over next, and any unease about the sea witch's magic slipped away.

"Do not tell anyone of your travels in the sea. I have no business with your people, so they have none with me. Our worlds are better left separate." Alana's voice echoed around us while we were still held by the water.

Wind knocked us around until we fell onto the warm sand. I opened my eyes to find the later afternoon sun beating down on us. Squinting, I rolled over and inspected myself to find I was dry and unharmed.

Alana might have thought our kinds had no business with each other, but I had a feeling that wouldn't be the case forever. If she was bonded to a fae that she intended to bring back to life, I had no doubt we would see her again.

"Is everyone okay?" Finn asked as he stood up.

Neva and Maddox nodded as we all wiped the sand off.

"Where are we?" I asked.

The beach around us didn't look like the one we'd entered the sea at. The sand was whiter, reflecting off the sun in almost a painful way, and it was hotter here than I'd ever felt on the main islands. The trees behind us weren't lush like North Island, either.

"We must be on one of the tourist islands," Maddox answered.

Gods, I'd always hated those. Centuries ago, our kind had created the fae realm to keep our people safe from the shifters and vampires; then, we began letting them in for a price. It was asinine. There was no item worth risking the drama other supernaturals could bring here, in my opinion, but the royalty had always insisted it was a way to bridge the gap between the races. I was certain it was complete bullshit.

Branches snapped behind us, and a growl sounded. I expanded my wings and took a step forward as a big ass wolf shifter stepped out of the trees. His silver fur had a black undertone that deepened his overall color. I met his forest-green eyes and ignored the sharp teeth he snapped at us as he got closer.

His growls lessened, and he stopped snarling once he touched the sand, but I was still leery while we waited to see what he would do.

"Should we just leave?" Neva asked.

Finn shook his head. "The sea witch might have dropped us here for a reason."

Probably for her own entertainment, but maybe I was wrong.

The wolf began to shimmer, his fur turning to skin as he rose onto his back legs and turned into his human counterpart. Clothes appeared with him, but not much skin ended up covered. He wore only board shorts, telling me he was likely here for pleasure and not someone we needed to worry about.

"I was told I'd have this island to myself. I paid a hefty price for it." The shifter's voice was husky, as if he hadn't spoken in days.

"Well, we certainly didn't come here by choice," I replied, openly appraising him. Not too long ago, his green eyes, trimmed bronze hair, and muscles like a Norse god would have been a turn-on, but my newly acquired mate bond must have shut down that part of me. Instead, the whole situation made me more curious than anything.

He was throwing off some serious alpha vibes, and I wondered if he'd left a pack behind or been kicked out of one. Normal people didn't vacation alone and pay a *hefty* price for it.

"Are you by yourself?" Finn asked.

"I don't think that's any of your business, fae. Like I said, I paid for my stay on this island. It'd be best if you left," he said with a tone of authority.

Definitely an alpha.

"Easy, Wolfy. We didn't come here to ruin your pity party for one," I said.

"My name is Roman, not Wolfy, and I did not come here to be disrespected. I came to be alone, so I'd suggest you leave now." His tanned form started to shimmer around the edges as if he was fighting off a shift that he should have had more control over.

"Not much of an alpha if you can't even keep your

wolf in check," I added, because I also had a problem with control. Except mine was over my mouth.

Roman took two steps closer to me, and Finn stepped between us. "My mate doesn't mean to threaten you. She just doesn't know how to keep her thoughts to herself. Our troubles are not with you. We'll be going."

When he'd called me his mate, my heart did a weird flip-flop in my chest, but I didn't pay as much attention to that as I did the ache in the shifter's eyes.

"Running from something?" I asked, because I'd seen it in my own.

"Something like that," he replied gruffly.

"Well, if you want to take any aggressions out, you're welcome to come with us," I added. Given Roman hadn't attacked us, he probably really was there just to get away and we'd been the one to interrupt him.

He shook his head. "I don't think that would be a good idea."

"Great. Now that we've settled all that, can we leave?" Maddox asked with a huff.

Finn nodded. "Enjoy your stay on the islands, Roman. Just a warning, I'd stay away from the main one."

The shifter nodded and let his wolf rise to the surface. As much as I hated dealing with the overbearing shifters at times, I was always fascinated by watching them shift.

First, his eyes changed from human to wolf, still retaining their green color, but there was a primal effect to them as they transformed. Then, he bent forward, fur sprouting along his skin, and within a split second, he was back on four legs, standing about four feet tall with his head held high.

The wolf nodded at us one last time, then turned to race back into the forest. I briefly wondered what he was running from but reminded myself we had our own problems to handle. I didn't really care about shifter ones.

"Well, that was pointless," Maddox grumbled.

"It was something." Finn turned to Neva. "We're going to need your help getting us back to Maeve. Are you ready?"

She nodded, her dark curls even bouncier after having been in the water. "It will be easier now that we know what to expect."

I glanced up at the sun again and wondered how long we'd been gone. I wanted to be back at the castle by nightfall. We'd started our day early and, if all went as planned, it wasn't going to be ending anytime soon. Maeve better be ready to hold up her end of the deal.

With one last look around the sparse beach, we teleported back to North Island, arriving at just the wrong place and time.

Guards dressed in all the same garb fought against each other, and flames erupted around us. More of the island was burning. I didn't know what Zephyr's fascination with fire was, but it needed to stop. He was destroying the realm that was supposed to be utopia for fae, and that was not okay.

"Why are they fighting each other?" Neva asked,

but none of us got the chance to answer as someone spotted us.

"Kill them!" a guard shouted and no longer were they attacking each other. Instead, all of the fae charged for us.

I grabbed Neva's arm and shoved her back. "Disappear. Now."

Without confirming she listened to me, I extended my wings as Finn and Maddox spread out next to me. "This is where you let go of that pain, Maddox," I reminded him, and he grunted.

"How are we going to get around all of them?" Finn asked, taking in the three dozen fae headed our way.

"We're not. We're going to go right through them," I replied.

CHAPTER 18

Finn didn't argue with me. Instead, the three of us readied, and I confirmed Neva was indeed gone, preferably in her little pocket realm where she would be safe from whatever was about to go down. I might've had no problem encouraging Maddox to become more like me, but after hearing about Neva's past, I was even more convinced that she needed to stay out of our fight.

Some of the guards began to fight again, but we still had no idea who was who. I assumed at least some of them were the Renegades dressed as royal guards in hopes of blending in. Clearly, that had failed, but until they got closer, we had no idea who was on our side, if anyone was at all.

"Keep that blood safe at all costs," I called to Maddox and then struck out with my magic.

Maddox beat me to the first few guards, though. He shook with unfiltered fury, his gossamer wings out and pushing him forward faster than I thought possible.

Finn was at my side, and I held him back, wanting to see what Maddox would do. He'd been holding a lot of aggression in over the last day, and we needed him to explode now instead of later.

"Focus on the ones further back," I said to Finn, even though I still didn't know which guards were fighting against us.

Finn didn't hesitate, and I followed him until one of the guards came at me.

"The king wants you alive, but I've come to learn he doesn't always know what is best." The fae curled his lips in a snarl, and I laughed.

"Then, maybe you should also know his enemies aren't necessarily yours," I replied, but he didn't seem deterred and moved to strike me.

My wing covered the front of me, taking the impact of his magic that vibrated my entire body. The fae was strong, but not more so than me. I lowered my wing and sneered at him, sending a blast of magic that knocked his ass to the ground. He was unconscious, but not dead. Two more fae headed for me, but these ones held their hands up.

"The king is looking for you. He has promised to burn everything until he finds you," one of them said.

"Well, then. I'll just have to find him first," I replied as I raised my left hand and sent a wave of magic into the idiot who thought he could sneak up behind me.

Glancing over, the fae was twitching on the ground, but what held my attention most was Maddox. He was moving in a near blur and beating the hell out of anyone he encountered. Some of the fae began to steer clear of him, and I assumed them to be Renegades. By the time I could turn back to the ones who had approached, there were none of the king's guards left to take care of. Most dead, the others having disappeared.

Only ten Renegades were left standing. I had no idea how many they'd shown up with; I doubted they'd had zero casualties.

"Where is Maeve?" I asked.

"She is keeping watch at home base. She protects our most important assets," a fae with a red band around his upper left bicep answered. His long ebony hair was pulled back into a ponytail, emphasized by a strong widow's peak, and his russet eyes were focused on me.

"Who are you?" Finn asked, likely noticing the same thing as me.

"I'm Maeve's second-in-command Orson. From the way she spoke, I'm surprised to see you back so soon," he said, still keeping an eye on me, which didn't go unnoticed by Finn who moved a little closer to me.

"Well, Orson. We are back. How about we go see Maeve so she can hold up her end of our deal," Finn said with a bite.

Oh, how I loved when he got feisty.

Maddox grunted in agreement with Finn, and I noticed he was still breathing hard from the adrenaline rush he likely experienced during the fight. Hopefully, it was enough to satisfy most of his rage at Ivy being taken.

Orson nodded curtly and turned without saying

another word. He disappeared along with the others without inviting us along.

"Maeve expected us to die in the sea. She made the blood oath, because she didn't have any plans of following through on it," I said as Neva popped back into existence.

"If she doesn't help us get in that castle, I will kill her myself," Maddox snapped.

Finn sighed. "Killing isn't the answer to all of our problems, brother."

Maddox huffed. "Well, your mate was right about it making me feel better."

"It's a temporary remedy. I promise you that," Finn replied with a pointed look at me.

They were both right. It was why I had continually searched out trouble back in LA. I needed the release of a fight to keep my darkness sated. Inner demons came in all forms. According to Olida, my biggest one had been manufactured and was no longer an issue after my bonding to Finn, but my past was still ever present.

I hadn't let go of my true anger, but I had sensed the changes in me even more after the bond. While I fought against them, I wasn't oblivious. I was slower to act in some things and more aware of others around me. Regardless, my new give-a-damn still didn't override my sense of self-preservation, and that didn't bother me one bit.

"Neva, can you get us back to the house? We should probably get there before Maeve tries to leave," I said.

"She won't be leaving her house. I made sure her blood oath was unbreakable. If Maeve does not hold up to her agreement, then she'll live out the rest of her days burning in pain," Neva answered.

"Is that what the part about 'blood boiling consequences' meant when you edited her words?" Finn asked.

Neva nodded. "Something about her is off. She was too willing to do the blood oath. For as knowledgeable as she seemed, it didn't sit right. An oath can only be broken in death. Since we didn't die, she either holds up her part of the bargain, or her blood will literally boil until she does."

Holy hell. Who was this elf, and where had she been my whole life?

I wrapped an arm around her. "Oh, you have no idea how proud I am of you right now."

"Ivy needs us. All that matters is that Maeve gets us to her." Neva grimaced, clearly not okay with her actions, so I held her tighter.

"Let's get moving, then," I said.

Finn led the way as we all disappeared, then reappeared in the forest. Neva stepped out in front of us, power already emanating from her.

"This way," she said confidently.

As much as I loved this Neva, there was a slight worry that my encouragement was going to break her, but maybe that wouldn't be such a bad thing. We were both changing and hopefully for the better.

Maddox followed Neva, and I moved to do the same, but Finn held me back. We hadn't really talked since leaving Mosi's island, and I kind of liked it that way. Besides the unexpected heat he'd thrown my way on the beach, the constant need to be on the move had given me space to think for myself again.

The bond was stronger than I'd anticipated. When I thought back on the few days that had passed, I realized how easily I'd let myself accept his touches and picture a future I'd never even thought twice about before.

There was a constant pang in my chest every time I pushed him away that I'd attempted to bury, but it only grew stronger as I avoided our situation. Finn, on the other hand, wasn't one to let things go, and the twitch in his jaw said we had unfinished business.

"How are you doing?" he asked first.

"Great. Life is working out just how I hoped."

He rolled his eyes. "How exactly did you tell Maddox to 'handle his shit'?"

"The same way I do. Unleash the pent-up emotions, but only on those who deserve it. Clearly, he's good at following directions from what we just saw." I tried to sidestep him and make sure Neva and Maddox didn't get too far ahead of us, but Finn tightened his hold on me.

"You know that isn't the only solution to people's problems, right?"

I nodded. "But it was this time. Can you be okay with that?"

He saw the challenge in my question and didn't back down. "I can, and I am."

"Are you sure?" I raised a brow at him, pausing my attempts to get past him.

"Positive. Our bond has shown me more than I was

willing to see before. I meant it when I said I accept you for who you are, Lucy. I won't ever lie to you, but it doesn't mean your actions won't frustrate me as we both adjust."

I patted him on the chest and tossed a saucy wink at him. "Then, we're on the same page. Just remember, angry sex is the best kind. I intend to push your buttons as often as possible."

He groaned, but it wasn't all in frustration. I might not be down with public displays of affection, but I wasn't going to deny our attraction, either. I liked Finn, and I wanted him. I just didn't know how far I was willing to take those wants. As long as he continued to be patient and understanding with me, then I would stick around to figure it out.

He surprised me by grabbing both of my arms just like he'd done on the beach. "You're killing me slowly, you know that?" he murmured against my neck as he breathed me in.

"But you're enjoying it," I replied with a smirk.

Instead of responding with words, he left a trail of fire along my skin as his hold on me tightened and I once again ended up with my back pressed against a tree.

"Picking up where we left off earlier?" I asked, voice husky with a need I didn't expect.

"The bond… do you feel it?" he murmured.

I knew exactly what he was talking about. The pull. The need. The emotions. All of it was pushing us together. It didn't matter that we were in the middle of the forest. We'd gone too long without touch, and the bond said time was up.

"I do, but Neva and Maddox could come back for us once they notice we fell behind." I was trying to convince Finn this was a bad idea, but my breathy words didn't hold much strength.

Magic hammered through my body as need like never before exploded within me, making me ache all over.

Finn's lips crushed to mine in a passionate kiss that had me clawing at his clothes, needing to be as close to him as possible. I didn't know much about bonds, but I was pretty sure continuing to have sex with him wasn't going to allow me to walk away from him. Though, those consequences were the last thing on my mind as his hands trailed down the front of my stomach and slipped beneath my pants.

"Clothes have got to go," I moaned, and he wasted no time complying.

Using magic to speed things along, we were both free of our pants within seconds, and there were no more gentle touches. Finn surged into me with one swift move, and my nails dug into his back as I arched, taking everything that he was willing to give.

"You are mine, Lucinda. I won't let you go," Finn grunted, and I wasn't sure if he was trying to convince me or himself.

I didn't respond with words. My mind didn't want to be there, and I wouldn't give him false promises. I let the bond continue to take over my actions and gave in to the euphoria he was pulling from me like he was an expert in all things Lucinda.

Every touch was purposeful, every kiss filled with a passion I didn't know existed. I closed my eyes, tilted my head back, and cursed the fucking bond, all while thanking the gods for allowing sex to feel this damn good.

Finn was going to ruin me, one thrust at a time.

I quickened the pace—my subconscious not forgetting we still had things to do like the bond had—and we finished together with throaty moans.

After we were done and I was able to focus on Finn's face, he was holding me gently, one hand spread under my ass and his other stroking my cheek. "You are mine," he repeated.

"You keep that up and you just might be right," I murmured, wanting nothing more than to curl up in a bed and sleep, but also knowing it wasn't possible. Not yet.

"As much as I wish we didn't have to, we should probably catch up with Neva and Maddox." Finn watched me closely as I nodded in response. Then, he added, "When this is over, I'm taking you to one of those islands where we can repeat this as often as we'd like without interruption."

A soft laugh left my lips. "You haven't seen enough of Earth. There are plenty of other places I'd rather be than within the fae realm once Zephyr is dead."

Finn grimaced, stepping back to grab our discarded clothes. I knew we were going to have a problem about my refusing to stay here when this was all done, but that wasn't something I was going to let either of us worry about yet.

I accepted my pants, finding my underwear inside them, but not seeing my shoes. By the time I was dressed, Finn was ready and holding my boots.

"In the trees." He smirked, handing them over to me.

A shudder caressed my skin as my mind did its best to fight the desire starting to build once again. As soon as my boots were back on, I moved to find Neva and Maddox and get back on track. I'm sure they hadn't missed what we'd been up to, and I appreciated that neither of them had interrupted.

It might have seemed selfish and reckless for Finn and me to spend those moments alone, but our bond made us stronger. Sometimes, it was worth it to be greedy. I already felt more energized as we trudged through the trees looking for our friends.

After several minutes of searching only with our eyes, I stopped and used my power to search out Neva's that seemed to grow the more she used it. Sure enough, I caught her trail and followed the magic she was putting off.

Finn stayed at my side and was back in warrior mode. His wings were out, and gone was the desire we'd both been lost to just moments before. "I don't like Maeve," he said.

"Yeah, neither do I. She's going to screw us over if she can," I replied, keeping my voice low as we finally spotted Neva and Maddox. They were only a few yards ahead of us now, and I didn't want to freak Maddox out with our doubts.

"Then, why are we going back to her?" Finn asked.

"Because she made a promise, and I'll be damned if I let her out of it after sending us on what should have been a suicide mission. After that, well, she can do whatever she wants. Except if she gets in my way, I'll kill her."

"Your mind, it's so black and white. How do you do that?" he asked without judgement.

I shrugged. "Anything in between was beat out of me long ago. People either make good choices, or they don't. They either need to be punished, or they don't. There isn't usually an in between."

"I might not always agree with you, but I'm beginning to see your point of view," he replied.

"Good, because I promise it will save your life one of these days. Maybe even sooner than you think."

CHAPTER 19

$\mathcal{M}$aeve was waiting outside when we arrived back at their hideout. She tapped her foot at the top of the porch, glaring down at us.

"What's wrong, Marcy? I thought you'd be happy to see us," I said, purposely using the wrong name again.

Her lips twisted into a forced smile. "Of course I am, but as you might have seen, I just lost some good men out there that were trying to stop our island from burning down. It hasn't been the best afternoon. I presume yours was better."

I grinned right back. "It was certainly interesting." She didn't deserve the details of our underwater adventure. If she wanted to know more, then she could swim her happy ass down there herself.

"Do you have what I've requested?" she asked, glancing at my empty hands.

My gaze met Neva's. I wanted her approval before we handed the blood over. The elf seemed to know more than I'd once given her credit for, and I trusted her to make the right call. Neva nodded, and I walked to Maddox, who was staring daggers at Maeve.

"Not now. Remember what I said. Revenge isn't always an instant gratification," I whispered as I held my hand out.

Love made people do stupid things. Maddox wasn't at all the same fae I'd met a few weeks ago. He'd learned that life was a bitch sometimes, and he wasn't handling that very well, but he had the potential to take control back. I could see it, and I hoped he did, too. I needed more people like him around if we were going to succeed at killing Zephyr.

Maddox handed me the ceramic container, and I wrapped my fingers around it gently. The liquid sloshed as I turned, and my palm heated from the magic within. I'd never met a siren. I didn't know anything about their kind. Any supernatural that was water based was thought to have been long ago dead, but now that I knew better, maybe I'd learn more about them.

Maeve met me at the bottom of the steps and held her hand out. She licked her lips, all too eager to get her hands on the blood.

Before I handed it to her, I stopped a few feet away. "I might not have been in the room when you took your blood oath, but Finn and Neva were. I don't care where your loyalties lie, or what you think about me. You made a deal. You will honor it, or you will burn in more ways than one. Do I make myself clear?"

She lunged for me, but I moved the blood away and

brought my hardened wing up, holding it just inches from her neck as she paused. "Don't test me, Macy. You won't like the results."

She hissed. "I am a woman of my word, *Linda*. Now, give me the blood and I will take you to the castle. I promised to get you in the door undetected, and that is what I will do."

"One wrong choice, and I won't hold my wing back next time," I added as I dropped the blood into her waiting palm.

"There won't be a next time," she sneered, bringing the container close to her chest.

"We'll see about that." Gods, I really hoped there would be, because killing her would make me oh so happy.

She turned on a heel and headed back inside, still holding the siren's blood close.

"Where do you think you're going?" Maddox called before I could.

Maeve turned back to us, her aqua eyes glowing bright in an unnatural way—even for supernaturals. "You have no idea what you've brought me. It needs to be locked away before I can leave. Wait here, and I will be back with two of my men to help escort you to the castle as agreed."

Hopefully, we hadn't just given her something that would destroy us, because she was right. I had no clue what power the blood held.

I walked back to the others. They all looked worried, possibly for differing reasons.

"This isn't going to work," Finn said.

"Probably not, but it's either we try this, or we storm through the front doors. I know there are more of us now, but look at how far that got me last time. I was consumed with rage and didn't let rational thought in. I'd rather not go that route again," I replied.

He smirked. "Rational thought, huh?"

"Just because our versions of rational are different doesn't mean I don't have any."

Maddox grunted. "So, she gets us in, and then what?"

All three of them stared at me. My plan had always been to focus on killing Zephyr. With the darkness gone from my head, I'd also spent a lot of time thinking about Ivy. The strength and acceptance of her fate was clear in Ivy's eyes when I'd seen her at the castle gates. It was something that I hadn't been able to forget.

She deserved to live. I knew that, but I was having a hard time putting her before my needs. Yes, I was aware that made me a shitty person. At least I was even considering it. I knew that was more than I would have done even a week ago.

"Until we see where Maeve is going to get us in at, it's hard to say what our plan should be. We'll either get Ivy out first or have to fight with the guards. If the chance to kill Zephyr comes first, then I'll take care of that while the rest of you go find Ivy. She'll be in one of two places."

"What about just getting Ivy out unnoticed and waiting until the king is in one of his vulnerable states like Maeve had mentioned, then coming back?" Neva suggested.

It wasn't a bad plan, and if it played out that way, I might be okay with it, but I wasn't making any promises. I hadn't mentioned it yet, but I also hadn't forgotten how the sword had powered me in an unnatural way. I needed to get my hands on it before I faced Zephyr. I had a feeling it was the key to my success. If we faced him and he wasn't aged, then I very well could be on another suicide mission.

"It's something to keep in mind. Like I said, let's see where we enter at before deciding," I said.

Maddox narrowed his eyes. "I don't care what happens or what your plans are. Just tell me where Ivy might be, and I'll take care of it."

I took a step toward him, meeting his challenge. "You won't do a damn thing until I know where we're going. If you make one wrong move, you could get us all killed. We will be outnumbered. Potentially, by fae who have no idea what they're doing and are probably there against their will. Do you want to be responsible for the deaths of your fellow fae?"

Maddox lowered his head, his height making him feel bigger and badder than me, but I was two seconds from showing him otherwise. "I don't care as long as I have Ivy."

"And if she looks at you like you're a monster and won't go with you after what you might need to do in order to succeed, what then?" I countered, my hands itching for a fight.

"She would never," Maddox said, but there was less bite in his voice. He was beginning to see reason.

"You keep telling yourself that, but I've killed

people in front of her before. Killed them to keep you, Finn, and her safe, but it made no difference. I was a monster to her when I was done." Satisfied that my point was made, I spun around to give myself some space.

It wasn't useful for any of us to fight with each other. As much as I used to believe I could do this on my own, I knew better after almost dying and losing the part of me that made me feel invincible. I wasn't afraid to die, but there were things I wanted to do before that happened. Ending the terror that was King Easton Zephyr was at the top of that list.

The sun was beginning to set, and I was grateful for that small fact. Sneaking into the castle would be a hundred times easier under the cover of darkness. Even still, we had more than a handful of challenges set before us.

Maeve came bounding down the stairs, a bounce in her step that hadn't been there before, and her eyes were back to their normal color. "Let's go."

"Where are the men coming with you?" Finn asked.

She tossed her hands in the air casually. "Oops. I forgot about them with all the excitement. I'll grab them." She disappeared into the house again, much too eager.

"I knew she wanted the blood, but it's like she just smoked the world's best joint," I said, even more on edge than before.

"It's the blood," Neva said.

"What about it?" Finn asked.

"Depending on what exactly she is, if she's already

used some of it, then it could have boosted her in ways she was not prepared for. Blood of other supernaturals typically isn't used for good intentions."

I grabbed her shoulder. "What do you mean 'depending on what exactly she is'? Isn't she fae?"

"I don't know. The longer we're around her, and watching her reaction to the blood, I believe she's part fae, but it wouldn't surprise me if she was something else as well," Neva answered.

Shit. Hybrids were dangerous. Like shifters but with less control. Their minds often went crazy as one side battled for control of the other. If Maeve was fighting with the magic within her, the blood we'd just given her might only make her more irrational.

I took a step back and inhaled deeply. Clearly, I was capable of growth. The old me would have lost my shit just then.

Maeve came back out, this time with two fae behind her. All three of them were dressed in blue garb like the guards of the king, and I glanced back at Maddox. "Want to fix the rest of us up? With all the new additions they supposedly have, it could give you longer to get to Ivy if we blend in."

He nodded and got to work. The process took less time than before since he wasn't changing our faces. I could have asked Maddox to do that as well, but saving his energy seemed more important.

Finn was closest to him, so Maddox started there, followed by Neva, who had wrapped her curls into a tight bun again after they'd sprung free back in the ocean.

I snapped my fingers at her. "No fighting for you. I still don't want you to have anything to do with killing. Especially not after—"

She cut me off. "I'm going to be fine, Lucy."

Finn glanced between the two of us, confused. I didn't think Neva would be okay with me filling him in while the others were around, so I kept my mouth shut.

Maddox finished changing my clothes but didn't move away. "Want me to at least do something about your hair?"

"That's probably a good idea. Something short and dark," I replied.

He nodded and within seconds, my indigo locks were nowhere to be seen. I lifted my hands and felt an A-line cut. Pulling the hair forward as far as it would go, I grinned at the obsidian strands. "Very good, Maddie."

When we were all changed and wearing the hideous navy-blue outfits, we strode casually to Maeve. We might have been waiting for this moment for a couple of days, but Maeve had pissed me off, and she was on our terms now.

By the time we reached her, the overly happy fae she'd been minutes before was gone and in her place was the bitch we'd been dealing with.

"I don't have all day," she complained.

"Yeah, and I didn't want to take a swim in the ocean. Deal with it, Marge," I tossed back at her.

She ignored my jab and began moving her hands. I glanced at Neva since she'd been the one to consider

Maeve wasn't only a fae. Neva was watching her closely, and I tried to keep an eye on both of them.

Within moments, Maeve opened up a portal. Something fae definitely couldn't do. She stepped through it without looking back, and her men followed.

Neva met my stare and mouthed, "Witch."

Witches were sneaky bastards, and I was not happy about this, but instead of calling Maeve out, we all stayed quiet and moved through the portal. She stared at us, waiting for a comment, but thankfully, Finn and Maddox had caught on and kept their mouths shut.

"After you." I smiled and put my hand out once we were all standing in a forest I assumed was just beyond the castle.

Maeve sneered in what seemed like disappointment but moved on.

It was less than a minute later that we stopped. There were no buildings or castle in sight. "What are we doing?" I asked.

"This is where we part ways," Maeve said confidently.

I stepped into her personal space. "I don't think so."

CHAPTER 20

Maeve squared her shoulders at me, silver hair swirling with magic and eyes glowing in the darkening evening. She pointed to what appeared to be a discarded piece of wood covered by dead brush. "I got you to the entry. That was the deal."

I glanced back at Neva. "Was that how it was worded?"

She shook her head. "Maeve is to get us inside the castle unless you choose not to have her help all the way through."

Hmm, did I want her help? More importantly, could I trust her word that whatever this entry was would get us inside?

Deciding it wasn't just up to me, I turned to Finn and ignored the daggers that Maeve was throwing at me. Whatever her oath was, I assumed it meant she couldn't hurt us, or she likely would have already.

"What do you think?" I asked Finn.

He was keeping an eye on Maeve even as he

answered me. "If she is required to tell us the truth about this entrance, then I say we don't need her."

"If she doesn't get us to an entrance that will honor her word, she will suffer greatly," Neva answered before I could ask for confirmation.

"Well, that settles things. Where does this lead?" I asked Maeve.

Her jaw tensed as if she didn't want to answer, but I could tell she had no choice. Whatever this blood oath was, it was ironclad. I would have to remember that for future dealings.

"It will take you through an underground tunnel that leads to an old cellar beyond the cells. It's not used anymore and will put you within the castle walls undetected as promised. I am not responsible for whatever happens after you enter the cellar," she said through clenched teeth.

Neva stepped forward and offered her hand to Maeve. "Your honor has been kept."

I scoffed at that. I was pretty sure this woman had no honor, but I let them keep their formalities and moved aside as Maeve and Neva shook, finalizing the oath. There was a weird glow between their hands, then they parted.

Maeve sneered at me. "I didn't really expect you to come back from the waters."

I smiled in return. "I know. Too bad I'm not that easy to kill. Something you should remember. What I don't understand about you and Edgar is that we all hate the king. We didn't have to like each other, but we sure as hell could have worked together and dealt with the rest later. Instead, the two of you had to act like idiots. Take this as my promise. If you fuck with what we're doing here today, I will find you, and things won't be pretty when I do."

Maeve didn't flinch; she held my stare and nodded, which was more than I expected. "I hear you, Lucinda Morrow. Loud and clear. We'll be seeing each other." Then, she snapped her fingers and disappeared along with the two fae she'd brought with her.

I swiveled around to the others. "Did that bitch just threaten me back?"

Finn and Neva grimaced while Maddox nodded with a gleam in his eyes. I'd rubbed off on him a little too much. Fairy boy really needed Ivy back at his side to balance his ass out.

"I think she did," Maddox replied.

"Something to worry about later. Let's see how much fun this tunnel is going to be." I kicked the brush out of the way as Finn bent down to find a handle.

He yanked then glanced up at me. "It's locked."

"Well, then use your muscles and break it open. It's not like we give a shit if anyone else gets in, right?" I asked.

He shrugged. "Depends on why they're coming."

"True, but that's merely a potential problem for future us," I said.

Finn's brow pinched together. "We're starting to stockpile those future problems."

"Eh, I said *potential*."

He nodded and gripped the rusted handle with both hands before giving it a jerk. The hinges groaned as the wood splintered. Within a matter of seconds, the entire covering broke into dozens of pieces.

Finn tossed the bits he could to the side and pulled the brush back. "We can at least cover it back up when we're inside. Looks like there's a ladder."

Neva stepped closer, a ball of magic in her hand illuminating the area around us with a soft glow. "Something to help lead the way."

I nudged her. "What other tricks do you have up those sleeves?"

She only smiled at me and dropped the ball of light down the hole, then moved aside. "After you."

"Uh huh. Don't think when this is all over that I'm going to let you go back to the way things were," I said as I moved toward the opening.

"Oh, I doubt anything after this will ever be the same, but I look forward to it nonetheless, Ms. Lucinda." She winked as I glared at her for the formalities that I'd thought we'd finally moved past.

Now that I was getting to know her even better, I was pretty sure the elf had purposely been proper with me just to irritate me the last couple of years. She was evil in an adorable package, and I kind of liked it.

Finn reached his hand out to help, and I hesitated. "Did you want to go first?" I asked.

"I think you're more than capable of handling anything that could be down there. I'll be last to make sure everything is good up here," he replied.

I took his offered hand and winked at him. "Maybe I'll reward you later for your progressive thinking."

"And maybe I'll let you." He grinned in return.

That was as affectionate as I was going to get while the others were still around. Given I could see the light Neva dropped down, it didn't appear too far. I jumped into the hole without using the ladder.

My legs bent, and I landed on the dirt ground with a soft thud, then coughed as dust swirled around me. The opening was only about four feet wide and Neva was already on her way down, so I moved out of the way, hitting my head on the ceiling.

Well, this was going to be fun. The stupid tunnel was less than six feet tall. We were going to be hunched over the entire way if things didn't change as we traveled closer to the castle. All of us except for Neva that was.

She moved to stand next to me when she got down. "Comfortable?"

"Did something give you the impression that I wasn't?" I asked in return with a fake smile.

Maddox joined us before she could answer, and Neva picked up the light as we squeezed together, waiting for Finn.

"This is pleasant," Maddox complained, but there was an underlying excitement to his voice that hadn't been there since Olida's juju had been influencing him.

Finn jumped to the bottom and turned around. His head was nearly a foot higher than the ceiling we were crammed under.

Without complaint, Finn bent down to a knee. "Lucinda, you should lead the way. We don't know if Maeve lied about where this will lead. Oath or not, I still don't trust her. We go in assuming there is an army waiting for us."

My lips moved into a smile on their own. Not because I felt that Finn was becoming more like me, but because he was being realistic. It was unfortunate his world had to come tumbling down around him for that to happen, but he'd fought reality for much too long.

"I'm good with that. I want Maddox behind me, then Neva, and Finn, you can watch the back," I suggested.

Nobody objected, and considering I had no idea how long it would take us to get wherever we were about to end up, I didn't wait any longer to start moving. There were no identifying markers as we moved slowly through the tunnel, everyone but Neva wincing when we tried to stretch even a little.

Red dirt clouded around us, likely worst for Finn since he was last, but nobody complained as we continued. I held Neva's ball of light in my hand, surprised to find the orb stayed cool and bright even after half an hour.

Finally, the ceiling began to get taller and, while I couldn't stand straight yet, I only had to keep my knees slightly bent to avoid impact.

Another ten or so minutes passed, and the tunnel opened even more. We were all clear of hitting our heads, even the giant Finn.

Nobody talked as we continued to move, but this time, grouped closer together. Power hummed around all of us. Even Neva was ready for a fight, much to my dismay. I mainly wanted her around to keep watch over

Ivy if we found her and couldn't get out without a fight.

A metal door appeared in front of us. It was old as hell, rusted, and had no handle. "Well, this looks useful," I droned.

Neva pushed forward and placed her hand on the steel. "There's no magic pulsing through it. We should be able to use brute force to get past it."

I laughed. "'We' as in one of us and not you."

She shrugged. "Sure, that works, too."

"Closet badass," I muttered as I felt around the edges of the obstacle before us.

I wasn't familiar with the lower levels of the castle. Only the prison, but even that was on a limited basis. Most of the people I was sent after didn't live long enough to see the inside of a cell, but there were occasions when it was necessary to keep someone alive long enough to get them talking.

Finn joined me, and we worked together. Maddox was bouncing on his heels, annoying the hell out of me with his fidgeting that kept distracting me in my peripherals. Finally, the rust began to crack, and the groan of metal sounded.

We all froze and paused all movements to listen. The door was cracked, and cool wind came through from the other side, but there was no noise or light.

"Shall we?" I said softly to Finn, keeping my voice low in case sound carried.

He nodded, and we pulled on the door again, slow and steady to keep the sounds to a minimum. When the opening was only about two feet wide, we stopped. I took the light back from Neva and tossed it inside the room.

I waited several seconds again before peeking my head in and was disappointed to find it was actually an old wine cellar. Nobody waited for us. There was nothing but cobwebs and bottles of alcohol.

"Well, that was anticlimactic," I grumbled as I stepped inside first.

Finn was right behind me, his sigh of relief audible. "Where do you think this is within the castle?"

"I'm not sure. We just have to keep moving and hope we start going up at some point. Ivy will either be in the dungeon, which is just a bigger set of rooms near the cells, or she's being kept in a room near Zephyr's chambers," I answered, glancing around the cellar to see if there was anything we could use.

Neva picked up a bottle of wine and dusted it off, reading the label.

I gave her a small nudge. "You picked a great time to take up drinking."

"Well, I figure nobody knows who I am, and if I can get away with it, I could say I was bringing the king a celebratory bottle of 1796 Lenox Madeira. If they didn't believe me, I could always smash it against someone's head as a distraction."

I had no argument with that. At least she had some sort of plan for staying out of the action while still remaining present, because I doubted we could do this without all of us playing some sort of role. Even if I didn't like having her in danger.

Maddox moved to the second door first. "Can we continue now?"

Finn didn't object, and I certainly wasn't going to. We each moved forward, and Maddox carefully opened the door that led to another hallway, and this one remained normal-sized. Though, it was still dingy. I was thoroughly surprised Maeve hadn't screwed us over. I was positive we'd be walking into an ambush, but so far, things seemed easy. Actually, too easy.

Maybe it was a sign we should slow down, but that would have taken the fun out of the shitty situation. So, I didn't say anything as we all pushed forward, staying quiet. Well, until Neva sneezed, and someone shouted from up ahead.

A light shined down toward us, and I smashed the one Neva had created.

The others moved to the side, but I stayed put.

Things could only get better if Gabriel was coming and I could rip his ugly ass head from his body right after I stole his delicious sword.

CHAPTER 21

The light from whoever was walking toward us disappeared, and I waited for my eyes to adjust. I could see the silhouette of a man, but there was nothing identifying to help me figure out if I knew the fae coming or not.

Warmth covered my back as I sensed Finn through our bond that I'd been damn good at ignoring since we left Mosi's island—except for in the forest. His hand wrapped around my hip as he let me stay right where I was. I didn't think having his support would mean anything, but the way my chest tightened at having him near was telling a different story.

That was something I'd have to sort out later. The footsteps from the approaching fae were too close, and I readied my hands for a fight. The hallway wasn't wide enough for me to use my wings, but I always packed an extra blade or two for situations like this.

Without waiting any longer, I leaped and landed on the fae without making much noise. I wrapped one hand around his mouth and the other at his neck as I swung my body around his back and whispered in his ear, "You're going to die."

He shook his head, words trying to escape through my hold.

Finn stepped closer, and Neva created another light. Maddox pushed past them both, eyes wide. "Lenny?"

The fae nodded beneath me as my blade began cutting into his skin. I glanced up at Maddox. "How do you know him?"

"I've met him here while bringing in goods. He has a farm, or had one, on South Island. I hadn't seen him in a while."

"That doesn't help me. Unless he has any usefulness to us, I'm going to kill him," I said to nobody in particular, keeping the dagger from cutting any deeper. For the moment.

Finn stepped forward, eyes charcoal and jaw tight. "What do you do for the king?"

I removed my hand from his mouth and placed it to his forehead, keeping my hold tight in case I didn't like his answers. It would only take a half-second to slice the blade through his throat.

"I've been here for a few weeks. When my crops died, my wife and daughter left for Earth. They said there was nothing here for us. I sent them ahead of me, promising to join them in the South hemisphere somewhere, but as I was packing the last of our things, Gabriel showed up. He said the king needed all of his men and I would either comply or die."

I wanted to tell him then he should have chosen to

die, but I'd once been in his spot. Though I was practically a kid, I'd known better and still complied.

Lenny continued, "I thought I'd only be here a short time, but things are getting worse. I haven't seen beyond the castle walls since my arrival. Do you guys know what is going on out there?"

I released my hold on him since he wasn't even trying to fight me and moved so I could see his face. The eyes could often tell more than words, and Lenny's were nearly lifeless and a dull blue.

"We're what's going on," I said while taking in the rest of his nondescript traits: buzzed black hair, slight shoulders, and thin waist.

"Have you seen a blonde woman that's being held here?" Finn asked when Lenny didn't respond to my comment.

Lenny shook his head. "Gabriel doesn't let most of us 'see' anything. We're just supposed to watch for people who don't belong. You're the first I've seen since my arrival."

Damn it. That wasn't helpful.

"Where are we?" I asked.

"At the rear of the castle. Above us should be the guard chambers and up ahead is storage. I haven't been beyond that, but I believe it's the holding cells. I've heard screams from there on many nights. Not much sleep happens here," Lenny answered.

Maddox's chest rumbled. "We need to get past here. How many more guards patrol these parts with you?"

"Probably another three on shift right now. But most of us don't want to be here. We were farmers just trying to provide a safe home for our families. We didn't know we couldn't trust our own king until it was too late."

Pity for the fae filtered into me, but it didn't change anything. We needed to keep moving. "Thanks for the information, Lenny. We'll be seeing you around." I turned to move, expecting the others to follow, but Lenny grabbed my arm.

I raised a brow at him. "I'd release me if you want to keep your head attached to your body."

He jerked his hand away and apologized. "I just wanted to know how you got in."

"Why?" Finn asked.

"So I can get out."

I laughed. "I don't think so. We're not helping you unless you want to help us."

"He already did. He let us pass and told us where we were. That is more than he had to," Neva spoke up.

I rolled my eyes and sighed. "Whatever. You guys can do what you want with him now, but next time, there will be less questions and more action."

Finn followed me as I moved to continue, and he was vibrating next to me. "What's wrong?" I asked.

"I left my sister here." His voice was rough and full of agony.

Understandably so. These lower parts of the castle weren't maintained. It was amazing the building hadn't fallen in on itself yet. The mostly brick and cinder walls were cracked and covered with spider webs. The air was stale, and the stench of death wafted through the cold air. We were two or three levels below ground, and everything was damn depressing. Add in the fact that

Ivy was being tortured, and well, that made it one hell of a nightmare.

I grabbed on to his elbow, encouraging him to focus on the task at hand instead of how long it took us to get to her. "You did what you had to. Ivy understands her role in all this. Just focus on the fact that she's not dead. We're going to find her."

He paid me no attention as he stared in front of us. "She's not dead *yet*."

If none of that helped, then there was nothing else that I could say to make him feel better, so I stopped talking. He had a right to be furious if he wanted to be. Those emotions could even be the key to saving his sister. We'd both done all we could considering the shitty situation. Now, it was time to see how it all played out.

Maddox and Neva joined us, no Lenny in sight when I glanced back. It wasn't like me to let people get away, but I was evolving. Look at me go.

Finn led the way this time, and we made it to another door without seeing anyone else. He didn't wait before opening it but did so quietly. Again, there was no one around. My gut was telling me this was wrong. We weren't supposed to be wherever we were, but none of the others were concerned, so I let my feelings go as my past caught up to me again.

The next hallway was made from cinder blocks and twice as cold as the cellar had been. An instant wave of nausea came over me, and a stabbing pain in my head made me stop to press my palms against my forehead.

I had no idea what was happening, but sickness like

this had never happened to me. Finn grabbed on to my arms, and I thought he was speaking, but I couldn't hear over the pounding in my mind. He turned me around and covered my hands with his own, forcing me to look at him.

I focused on his eyes, the bond that was hammering against my core, and the feelings he evoked within me. Slowly, the pain subsided, and my hearing returned.

"Lucinda?" he asked quietly.

"I don't know what happened, but I think I'm fine now," I replied, stepping closer to him and trying to soak up whatever energy he was putting off.

Finn nodded and took my hand, keeping me close. For once, I didn't mind.

We came to the first row of cells, and a tsunami of death rolled over us. I gagged and brought my shirt over half my face while scanning the area. Apparently, people were sent down here to die, and nobody bothered to clean up after it happened.

The first cell had three bodies in it, one definitely older than the other two. The second had four on the ground and a fifth newer one hanging from the ceiling. The smell must have been too much, and I didn't really blame him. One minute down here, and it would have been clear what his fate was.

Neva was in tears, and Maddox stayed near her, his face red with rage. "If Ivy is down here…"

He didn't need to finish. We all knew how much it would have ruined her on top of whatever abuse she'd already been served.

We continued down the long section of cells.

Thankfully, the worst of them had been where we started, but none of that mattered. There was no one alive down there. Only cold bodies and a few remaining empty cells they probably used to taunt prisoners with as they threw them in with the dead. The only benefit to finding nobody alive was that we didn't have to deal with some idiot yelling for us to set them free and bringing unwanted attention.

There was a sound from further up, but I couldn't make out what it was. Finn began to squeeze my hand tighter until it was almost painful. Before I could ask what was going on, he let go without warning, and the stabbing sensation returned in my head. I reached for him, but he wasn't next to me any longer. He was running away from where I stood with Maddox right behind him, but I couldn't follow. I couldn't even force words to leave my mouth to ask Finn to come back.

My muscles tightened and screamed as my insides heated. The warmth was first welcome against the cold air of the dungeon, but everything became too hot. I seized up, dropping to the ground. Neva joined me, reaching for my hand, but winced when her fingers touched my skin.

"Lucinda?" she asked.

I groaned, unable to give any other response or even focus my eyes on her.

"Have you touched anything since we've been here?" she asked.

My head shook, or, at least, that was what I was going for.

"What exactly did Olida say about your darkness? I know it hurts to talk, but I need to know."

I took a deep breath in, and another out, then repeated several more times as Neva held on to me, but no matter how tightly she squeezed, her touch did nothing like Finn's. Where the hell was he?

Finally, I forced the words out to answer Neva's question, but I was nearly out of breath by the time I was done. "She said my bond with Finn made it go away. Freed me from some sort of curse Zephyr put on me as a child to make me a dark fae when I'd been born neither light nor dark. Apparently, he thought that would make me easier to control."

"A curse? You weren't cursed, Lucinda. I would have known it. Your darkness was strong, but it was part of you. I wasn't surprised when I couldn't sense it after the bond, but I didn't think it had truly gone away. Do you not feel it anywhere within you?" she asked.

I thought about her question, trying to ignore the roar of agony taking over my body. My skin took on a sheen from my efforts as I struggled to stay conscious. "I think I can feel the darkness but only sometimes. I don't hear it anymore."

By the time I finished speaking, I was damn near tears. My body shook against the grimy ground covered in Gods knew what, but I couldn't deny that the cold stones did ease some of my aches. Though, not anything like Finn had. If he didn't get back soon, I was going to haunt him for the rest of his miserable life.

Neva lifted my head with one hand and placed the other over my chest. "I don't think Olida knew what she was talking about, or she lied to you. I think the voice was forcefully suppressed and it's trying to come back out. That was not a curse in the sense someone gave it to you, Lucy. You're going to have to set the darkness free, or it's going to keep hurting you."

Her statement made me want to scream at her, but I knew none of this was her fault. Neva was the only person in my life who'd never lied to me. Sure, she'd omitted things about her abilities, but that didn't matter to me, because I knew she also accepted me just as I was. Sure, she hoped I'd make different choices at times, but I never felt ashamed for the things I did. If I figured out a way out of this shithole in one piece, I was going to make sure she knew how much I appreciated her.

As my mind fought to focus on her request, I closed my eyes and searched within me for the voice I missed. Still, there was nothing I could find to make a difference in my situation. Nothing tangible to set free.

"There's nothing there for me to grab on to. I don't know if you're wrong, or if there is something worse going on with me. Either way, Finn seems to be the only thing to make the pain stop. Do you think he did this somehow?" I hated to think that way, but the bastard had run off on me without a word and hadn't come back when we didn't follow.

Neva's eyes narrowed, and her head shook adamantly. "Finn would never. Olida must have done something when she healed you. I can't sense her magic on you, though. So, it might not have been on purpose, or she's even stronger than any of us realized.

Regardless, whatever is happening to you, I don't know how to fix it."

If Olida had anything to do with the way my body was revolting against me, I was going to torture the hell out of her. Her mischievous lavender eyes flashed in my mind, and I grew more furious by the second. This was why I didn't get close to others. They were almost always only out for themselves. I'd known from the start that Mosi and Olida had their own agenda, one they'd somehow convinced me was okay to keep secret.

Well, that wasn't going to work for me any longer. We had to get the hell out of the castle until I figured out what was happening to me. I wouldn't be able to fight in my current state, and contrary to how hard I'd fought to stay last time, I didn't actually have a death wish.

As I struggled to regain control of my legs, Maddox came back. His wings were out and eyes wild with emotion. "We found Ivy. She's not conscious, but she's alive. Finn is trying to free her from the cell." Then, he realized I wasn't okay. "What happened?"

"Nothing we can fix here. Go help Finn, so we can leave. I'm going to start getting Lucinda back to the tunnel," Neva answered, and I wasn't going to argue. We knew how to get inside, and we'd be back. Hopefully, within the next couple of days. The extra time could possibly give us the opportunity to get through to someone on the inside as well.

When Neva grabbed on to me, I tried not to laugh. She was more than a foot shorter than me, and her attempts to manhandle me weren't working so well.

But, she was determined and clearly not giving up, so I kept my thoughts to myself.

When her first plan failed, Neva released me back onto the repulsive floor and rubbed her hands together until they glowed red. Then, she put them on my stomach and head. Within seconds, the roaring sensation dulled to something still painful, but manageable in comparison.

"That likely won't help for long, but can you at least walk now?" Neva asked.

My legs were twisted under me. I leaned forward onto my hands, trying to straighten everything out. Gods, this was even more agonizing than when I'd had my stomach cut open and had a broken wing.

Regardless, I pushed through and, with the help of Neva, stood up after several choice words. By the time we were headed back the way we'd come, I was sweating profusely from the exertion, and I could hear the pounding of feet from behind us.

"It's just Finn and Maddox. They have Ivy," Neva said before I could try to look myself.

Perfect, because I was damn near ready to volunteer myself to whoever was coming just so they'd kill me and end my suffering.

We'd only made it another ten feet before Finn and Maddox caught up to us. Maddox was carrying Ivy, and Finn came straight to me.

"I'm so sorry I left you. I had to get her out," he said as his arms wrapped around me. The relief was instant. The change was so significant that I collapsed in his arms, but I righted myself before he could think to pick me up.

The searing heat was replaced with a cool stream of magic that I could only assume came from our bond. As much as I appreciated having some sort of control back, I wasn't pleased that it was at the mercy of Finn staying glued to my side. Once we were outside of the castle walls and the blocks they kept up, we'd be able to teleport away. Figuring out how to get me back to normal was the priority.

"Can I do anything more?" Finn asked, his eyes moving between me and Ivy's limp body in Maddox's arms. I couldn't see anything more than her matted hair from where I stood, and I was okay with that.

"Just don't let me go until we get back to Mosi's island," I replied all the while thinking about my revenge if Mosi and Olida had anything to do with how I was feeling. "I need to be at full strength when we confront them."

"What are you talking about?" he asked, but I waved him off.

"Not now. Let's just get the hell out of here."

It still took every ounce of energy I had to keep a moderately fast pace with them, but I was at least moving on my own even if I winced each time Finn's hand loosened slightly from mine.

Maddox and Neva were ahead of us and he froze after opening the door to one of the rooms just before the cellar. He took a step back, still holding on to Ivy and pushing Neva to the side. The area beyond the door was dark, so I couldn't see what made them pause.

A light flashed in my eyes, bringing spots to my vision as Finn backed us up further away from the dark room. Unease settled over me, and I instinctively called on my power. Even if I couldn't find my inner voice, it didn't mean I was defenseless. Or, so I hoped.

As my magic surfaced, Finn's grip on me loosened considerably and he growled in pain. "What the hell, Lucinda?"

I sighed. Clearly, nothing was going to go right for me within these walls. "Well, it's not like I meant to hurt you."

I was up shit creek without a paddle or even a damn boat if I couldn't let Finn go without collapsing and couldn't use my magic without hurting him.

Lenny came into view, and I breathed a sigh of relief. Maybe he'd had a change of heart and came back to help us. Except that thought diminished as soon as I saw the glint of a blade at Lenny's neck and five other fae stepped out of the darkness.

"Lucinda. I was hoping I'd run into you."

CHAPTER 22

Gabriel stood behind Lenny, and a fury rose within me. I wasn't sure what I was capable of in my current state, but I knew I couldn't fight him while holding on to Finn the entire time. Whatever was about to happen was either going to be a hot mess, or… actually, I couldn't see any other outcome.

Finn forced us to take a step back as Gabriel pressed forward with four more guards moving in around him. We were outnumbered and, given my current state, severely outpowered. I didn't care how much it cost me; I wouldn't give up willingly. Gabriel would never get me alive.

"I had hoped we'd killed you last time, but torturing you will be worth the disappointment you always seem to bring," Gabriel said, one of his hands choking Lenny and the other pointing a small dagger to the fae's neck.

"You won't live long enough for that," I replied, keeping my head up and refusing to show weakness, no matter how dire our situation seemed.

He tsked. "Oh, Lucinda. I know you. I helped create you. You're not who you think you are, and you can't win this. You should have stayed away if you wanted to live."

The other guards moved in closer. I didn't have much time to decide my next move. Maddox had moved behind us with Ivy still unconscious in his arms, and Neva was at my side, opposite Finn.

"Take her and go," I said to Neva. She couldn't bring anyone else to her pocket realm, but considering Neva was a lot more powerful than she'd allowed me to believe, I trusted her to find somewhere to hide with Ivy. Maddox just needed to be smart enough to trust Neva as well.

When I turned back to Gabriel, he smirked. "There is nowhere for you to hide. I won't let you get away from me again."

"I don't intend on getting away. I intend on killing you like I should have the last time," I sneered, power swelling within me, painful but not like when I'd collapsed. It was as if I just needed a release, like Neva said, and all would be fine, but I couldn't find the trigger to make it happen. Though, the longer we stood in this room, the more powerful I felt. Something was happening. I just had to survive long enough to figure out what.

Gabriel grinned. "Well, let's see how that works out for you. How about I start us out with the killing?"

Maddox shouted and began moving forward, having already given Ivy to Neva, but it was too late. Gabriel sliced open Lenny's throat and shoved him to the ground with a swift kick that sent Lenny crashing into the cinder wall. At the same time, the guards charged for us, and I had no choice but to let go of Finn. It was time to see how bad off I really was.

Finn's eyes met mine for the briefest of seconds, and I saw everything in him that I was feeling yet avoiding. Finn had made me care. He had changed me, and we'd brought out the best and worst in each other. He'd deserved better than the shitstorm brought on him.

Much to his dismay, I pushed Finn away as two guards came in at his right. Anguish swelled within me, but this time there was a pulsing energy along with it that was urging me toward Gabriel. That drive grew stronger than whatever had been trying to keep me down.

The space we were in was wide enough that I could unfurl my wings, but I had to be careful with them to avoid hitting the wrong people. Using my peripherals, I caught sight of Neva's tiny body standing over Ivy as her hands once again glowed red. The pain-in-the-ass elf hadn't listened, and I wanted to throttle her, but as magic caressed my skin that was not my own, I knew she was only trying to help.

Deciding I didn't have time to focus on Neva's stubbornness, I brought my wings forward and gave Gabriel my full attention. His upper lip snarled at me as he unsheathed his sword and tucked the smaller dagger away at his hip.

My chest blossomed with glee at the sight of the sword I'd thought about on several occasions since last touching it. The strength I'd felt wielding it was unlike anything I'd experienced before it. As the blade glowed with magic, I knew without a doubt I needed that weapon to kill Zephyr.

My muscles were starting to spasm again, but I was more intent on staying alive and put my focus on forcing my magic forward. Teal swirled around me as my wings hardened just in time.

Gabriel made the first strike and swung his sword around, the blade aimed right for my neck, but I blocked it with my hardened feathers. Dark magic flowed freely from the weapon in black swirls that intertwined with my own power. Instead of the hit hurting me like I expected, it energized me.

"I'm not easy to kill, Gabriel. Haven't you learned that by now?" I taunted.

"All the more fun for me," he replied, clipping the sword to his side before crouching down and ramming his shoulder into my gut.

I hadn't expected the close contact hit, and he threw me off guard, which allowed his momentum to carry us past the others fighting. My back slammed into a concrete wall opposite Neva and Ivy. I wrapped both hands around Gabriel's neck and sent a wave of power through him, but it was weak compared to what I knew I should have been capable of.

"Such a disappointment," Gabriel whispered as he reached for the dagger instead of using the sword that was warming my skin from the close contact.

"Yeah, I might be, but at least I'm not the king's bitch. You are nothing more than his pet, and I'd rather die than serve that bastard again." I shoved both hands into Gabriel's chest. Everything within me screamed, and I roared while calling on all the power within me.

Gabriel's body vibrated beneath my touch, and his eyes narrowed as he struggled to move against my magic, but even I knew it wouldn't hold long.

"I'm going to end you," he spat in my face.

"So you keep saying," I tossed back, feigning confidence as I felt my strength dwindling. I had to get my hands on the sword, but if I focused on anything other than keeping Gabriel at bay, I was as good as dead.

His arm raised just enough for his dagger to cut into my side. I tried to move left, but we were backed into a corner, and there wasn't room for me to get far enough away to avoid his hit.

As I hissed from the slash, my eyes caught sight of Finn several paces behind us. He'd already taken care of one guard, but the second seemed to be putting up one hell of a fight.

Maddox was near him, red faced, and I watched as he snapped the neck of a guard at the same time a wave of magic slammed into his back, keeping him preoccupied as he moved on to the next attacker.

It didn't seem as if I was going to be getting help from either of them anytime soon, but Neva was still near the back wall. Her eyes were closed, and she was pulsing with magic. I wondered if it was meant for me. After the initial boost I'd received from her, I hadn't sensed anything else.

"You know I might be a disappointment, but I'm

also full of surprises. Let's see how you like this one," I said to Gabriel, refocusing on my own fight.

I used what was left of my strength to slam my elbow down into the crook of his neck and went for the dagger in his hand. I ripped the hilt from his grasp and didn't hesitate before sinking it into his chest.

Instead of having the desired effect of shock and awe, Gabriel smirked at me.

"A few things have changed around here, Lucinda. I'm not that easy to kill, either," he said as he pulled the dagger from his chest and wiped his own blood off on his pants. Before I could try to move back, Gabriel repeated my same move, shoving the blade into my chest with enough force that I not only felt, but also heard my chest bones crack as he twisted the blade and pushed me to the ground.

Now that things were in motion, I realized it wasn't the smartest move I'd made, but I was intent on following through with it. Even if it didn't work out exactly how I hoped.

Finn roared and unleashed a wave of power unlike anything I'd ever experienced. "Lucinda!" he yelled right as he ripped the head off the fae he'd still been fighting. Blood sprayed across his face, but that wasn't what held my attention.

Gabriel's strike had missed its mark. My heart still beat strong in my chest even as everything around it was seared in agony. Finn grew stronger, and I was fascinated by the magic pulsing off him and calling to me. Gabriel must have sensed the shift in power, because his attention moved from me to the raging bull that was coming in from behind.

Even in Finn's charged-up state, Gabriel wasn't deterred. He reached back and yanked the blade from my chest. "I'm going to borrow that for a moment." He smirked down at me, then turned around to throw the dagger at Finn, who impressed me even more by catching it.

I leaned forward and reached for the sword at Gabriel's hip while he was distracted. As soon as I touched the glowing metal, my body was knocked back into the wall. My head hit first, taking the brunt of the impact, and my vision faltered as I tried to focus on what was happening with Gabriel and Finn.

Finn's light magic was tinged with a deep blue color I'd never seen from him when he fought. His eyes were dark in the center with a light ring of silver around them that glowed with intensity as he began exchanging blows with Gabriel.

I hated being weak. I needed to be the one fighting against that asshole. Not Finn. This was my battle. My demons to slay. Except Finn was doing it for me. I knew that I should be okay with it. That Finn was my mate, and he was only doing whatever it took to keep me safe, but that didn't stop me from moving forward.

I glanced at Neva, hoping for an assist from her, but her attention was elsewhere. Maddox was lying on the ground, and I gasped at the sight of him. His chest had a hole at the center that was much larger than my stab wound and something I wasn't sure he could recover from. Neva was leaning over him, her body rocking back and forth. Sparks of red flowed from her hands as she did whatever it was that she was capable of.

Realizing I was on my own again, I forced myself to move, but all I could do was crawl. My prize was within my sights, and I was only inches away as Finn and Gabriel fought by my side. I stretched my arm out but fell short from grasping the sword still hanging from Gabriel's hip, only managing to cut my hand on the tip.

He turned around and laughed, staring down at me. "Pathetic," he mocked, then kicked me in my ribs as Finn got in a hit of his own.

I rolled several times before I was able to stop myself. When I looked back up, Gabriel had Finn pinned against the wall, and the sword I'd been going for was now in Gabriel's hand, aimed and ready to take Finn's head off.

"I won't let you kill him," I muttered more to myself than anyone else, but Gabriel still heard me as I forced myself up.

He barely glanced my way. "You actually care for him. How sweet." Sarcasm dripped from his words, but I paid them no attention.

My hand pulsed with power, and I saw the dagger Gabriel had been using was carelessly dropped to the ground at some point. I picked it up as Finn rolled out of the way, dodging Gabriel's first swing of the sword. Blood trailed behind Finn, but given how quickly he'd moved, I tried not to dwell.

I got back on my feet, and the closer I moved toward Gabriel, the more strength I acquired. As this happened,

I knew without a doubt that the sword he wielded needed to be mine. I might have been consumed with darkness the last time I used it, but tapping into that side of me was going to be the only way for all of us to make out of the castle.

Before I could get to him, he changed directions and headed for Ivy. "You know, I've realized something. You obviously didn't come here to kill the king if you were already retreating after you got this peach. Let's see how you feel when I do this," Gabriel taunted as he pressed his open palm over Ivy's chest.

Ivy had been left unattended while Neva helped Maddox. I hadn't let that thought cross my mind during the chaos, but it was too late to do anything about it now.

Ivy's body convulsed, and her screams echoed around the room before they were cut off abruptly by the back of Gabriel's hand. Her head lolled to the side, vacant eyes open and staring at me.

No, this wasn't happening. Gabriel would not win. I couldn't let him get away again. Acting on pure instinct, I ignored the yelling around me and lunged forward without really thinking my movements through.

Gabriel stood, arms ready and waiting to grab a hold of me, but little did he know, I didn't much care what happened to me at that point, as long as he died.

I grabbed a hold of him, my legs wrapping around his waist as I used one hand to hold on to his neck and the other to control the dagger I held in my hand. I arced the blade up and I plunged it downward into the side of Gabriel's head. If the piece of shit didn't die by getting stabbed in the heart, then maybe a hit to his brain would do the trick.

As the tip of the dagger drove into his ear, Gabriel was at the perfect height to position the sword toward me. "I won't die without taking you with me," he said before the blade went through my top ribs and out my other side with no resistance.

My body seized, but not before I drove the dagger all the way to the hilt and Gabriel's eyes widened. He had probably been expecting me to back away to save my own ass, but in a moment of clarity, I accepted that this could be my fate.

We fell to the ground, Gabriel landing beside me, and I had the perfect view of Finn. Our bond flared to life, breaking through the last of the wall I'd built up when he'd been angry with me before, but it made no difference.

Darkness exploded from me as my heart slowed. The tug and pull of life and death waged a war within me as the tip of the sword cut into my arm when I tried to move.

Finn yelled for help as he made his way toward me, but I already knew there would be no pulling the sword out of my side. Heat consumed me, and flames of magic traveled along my skin and along the hilt in scorching fashion. I was being burned alive by the one thing I had thought would be exactly what I needed to win.

I warned that you wouldn't like what would happen if you suppressed me. This time, you're going to listen to me.

The inner voice was back, but it was too late.

Yeah, good luck with that. If you didn't catch on yet, I'm kind of dying over here, asshole, I replied as a heaviness settled over my body and my breathing slowed considerably.

You might want to die, but I won't let it happen, the voice demanded as a rush of frigid air caressed my senses and shocked my nerves.

My eyes opened of their own accord to find Finn hovering above me. Tears filled his eyes, along with a rage even I couldn't rival. His sister was dead, and it was my fault. Even if I lived, he would hate me.

"Is she okay or dying?" Finn demanded as warm hands felt around my chest.

Neva came into view next. "I don't know." Her voice was tense and filled with grief.

"They both can't die. Fix this, damn it," he growled as a roar echoed through the room.

I coughed up blood that splattered over my face as I tried to sit up. Finn's hands were on me in an instant, lifting my shoulders just a couple of inches off the ground.

Neva reached for the sword, but I yelled at her. "Don't touch it."

"How are you alive?" she asked, keeping her fingers just mere inches from the hilt.

"Probably because of the dark magic. Just give me a minute," I replied.

Alright, Darkness. What the hell is happening? Why am I not dead? I asked inside my head.

It's not our time yet. Take the sword out, but keep it close, and you will heal.

How? I asked even as I began doing just as it said.

You'll figure it out soon enough, was all I got.

I sighed, annoyed, but glad to be alive. As okay as I thought I'd be with only taking Gabriel out and then dying, I wouldn't have been. I needed to see the day King Zephyr took his last breath.

Carefully, I reached my arm up until my shoulder protested and grabbed the hilt with feeble strength. I pulled it out as far as my arm would reach before having to readjust and pinch the blade to free the remaining few inches still lodged into my ribs.

There was no pain associated with the movements, only peace. When I was done, I turned the weapon around and wrapped my palms around the black handle.

Power flared within me, and my inner voice sighed in contentment. *We are whole.*

I didn't know what it meant, and I didn't have time to question anything else before stomping feet headed our way.

"You should be dead instead of her," Maddox snarled, his shoulders heaving and bloodied hands shaking.

Neva must have done something to recharge him, because Maddox still had a gaping wound in his chest, but somehow had no problem controlling his motions.

Finn stood as I did, holding his hands out. "Lucinda didn't do this. Gabriel did, and he's dead. Next, we're going to kill Zephyr. They will all pay, but you need to put blame where it belongs, brother."

Maddox shoved him. "I'm not your fucking brother.

You've been on *her* side this whole time. You haven't given a shit about Ivy since you brought that whore into your home."

The metal of the sword warmed in my palm, but Maddox was not my enemy. I wouldn't hurt him as long as Finn could keep him under control.

My inner voice didn't agree, but as my strength increased, so did my ability to ignore it.

Finn grabbed on to Maddox and they continued to argue as Neva stepped into my view. "Your darkness is back?"

"It is."

Her lips thinned as she nodded but didn't speak her opinion. She glanced at Finn and Maddox. "I'm going to calm him down before he kills himself. I can't heal, but I did seal the injury so that he didn't bleed out. Only, it won't last if he insists on fighting more."

I nodded to Neva and set my sights on Ivy. Maddox must have moved her, because her head was facing up and body straightened out.

My chest burned with rage as I took the steps needed to get to her. I didn't know what I was doing, but I wanted to say goodbye in my own way. I wasn't close to Ivy. Hell, I had even been okay with her death, but that was when I thought it was necessary.

Nothing about how she died today was necessary.

I tucked the sword into my lap as I kneeled next to her. "I'm sorry, Ivy. You deserved better than this."

My hands grabbed hers where they rested on her stomach. She was still warm, still seemed so innocent.

The trait that had once disgusted me now filled me with sorrow.

Sorrow for the life lost and for the pain those who loved her most would have to find a way to deal with.

My hands glowed around hers, magic forming around us in a midnight-blue hue and coming from the sword. Sparks bounced around my hold on Ivy as I glanced at the others. Nobody was paying us any attention, and I had no idea what was happening.

Ivy's body began to tremble, then convulse as a golden light blocked out the darker magic and covered her prone form. She sucked in a deep breath and opened her eyes. They were no longer vacant, and I was speechless from shock.

How the hell had I done that?

"Your magic brought me back. I felt it everywhere," she croaked.

"I don't understand," I replied and tried to pull away, but she held on tighter.

"Lucinda, you did exactly what he wanted. You let the darkness back in."

Continue Lucinda's story in Dark Fae Unrivaled today!

Scorned by Blood

A New Adult Vampire series featuring a supernatural hunter and the sexy vampire bound to protect her no matter the cost.

Luna Marked

A complete New Adult wolf shifter series (dual POV) featuring a strong-willed leading lady and a patient, yet fierce alpha male.

Broken Court

A complete New Adult Urban Fantasy series featuring an unconventional and anti-heroine leading lady, a broody love interest, and a fae kingdom with a vile king.

Royal Fae Guardians

A complete Young Adult Urban Fantasy series featuring fae, magic users, a sweet romance, along with snark and humor.

Shadow Veil Academy

A complete Upper Young Adult Urban Fantasy Academy series featuring shifters, elves, witches, and more.

Elite Supernatural Trackers

A complete New Adult Urban Fantasy series featuring witches, demons, a smart-mouthed female lead, alpha males, and a snarky fairy sidekick.

Raven Point Pack Series

A complete Upper Young Adult Paranormal Romance series featuring wolves, witches, vengeance, and fated mates.

Blood of the Sea Series

A complete Young Adult Paranormal Romance series featuring vampires, open seas adventures, and the occasional pirate.

Standalone

Marked Paradox - A complete Young Adult Fantasy fae story about a realm divided and one fae to bring them back together.

ABOUT THE AUTHOR

Heather Renee is a *USA Today* bestselling author who lives in Oregon. She writes urban fantasy and paranormal romance novels with a mixture of adventure, humor, and sass. Her love of reading eventually led to her passion for writing and giving the gift of escapism.

When Heather's not writing, she is spending time with her loving husband and beautiful daughter, going on their own adventures. For more ways to connect with her, visit www.HeatherReneeAuthor.com.